BLIND BET

SUSAN HAYES

Some rules were made to be broken

Layla Corbin loves her life as a technician on the deep space asteroid-mining ship, Kessel Queen. Great job, great companions, great money. Perfect, except she wants all four of her sexy crewmates. The rules of the ship state she can only have one – an impossible choice.

When Mace issued that order, he did it to protect his crew. He never imagined that they'd all fall for Layla.

Note from the Author. This is the story that started it all. The first story I set in the Drift Universe, home of both the Drift and Nova Force series. This version of Blind Bet is a re-release with a new cover and revised/expanded content. Blind Bet is a standalone romance.**

COPYRIGHT

SUSAN HAYES

WEBSITE | NEWSLETTER | FACEBOOK

Blind Bet (Part of The Drift Series)

Release of this version: February 2019

Cover Design: Melody Simmons ~ ebookindiecovers.com

Editor: Dayna Hart

Published by: Black Scroll Publications

ISBN: 978-1-988446-44-8

DEDICATION

For my Mum and Dad, for always believing in me. And for Karen. My best friend, my sounding board, and provider of laughs and support.

This one is also for my readers. Thank you for coming on the adventure with me. When I wrote Blind Bet in 2013, I had no idea where this story would take me. The Drift universe is now one of my favourite worlds to write in, and I hope you continue to visit it with me for many years to come.

PROLOGUE

Out on the edge of civilized space is a rag-tag collection of space stations and platforms known as the Drift. It's a haven for the hunted, the lost, and those seeking second chances. The people who live there hail from every species, class, and corner of the galaxy, but they all have one thing in common: they don't belong anywhere else.

There's nothing beyond the Drift but wild space and an asteroid belt full of ore-rich rocks. The asteroids are mined by hundreds of vessels and their hard-working crews.

This story about one of those crews.

Welcome to the Drift.

CHAPTER ONE

"DAMN IT, I don't know why I play this *fraxxing* game with you bunch of cheats!" Layla Corbin dropped her cards on the dented metal table in disgust. She went to drown her sorrows with more of Jax's hooch, only to discover her mug was empty. "Great, I'm out of scrip *and* booze. This really hasn't been my night."

"You play with us because it's the only game in the sector and the only entertainment we have unless you want to spend another night watching vids." G'arn grinned at her from across the table that took up most of their cramped dining area and pushed a small stack of chips her way. "Jax, refill her drink before she gets really grumpy and tries to stab someone."

"No stabbing, Corbin." Mace snapped from the far end of the table. Mace was their crew chief and captain of the mining vessel they all called home. He narrowed his gaze at Layla until his sky-blue eyes were almost hidden behind his lids. "I'm not filling out another *vething* incident report because you yahoos can't play nice. Next one who requires a write-up is going to be sucking vacuum, because I will cheerfully throw any one of you out an airlock before I do anymore paperwork. We clear?"

"Damn, someone get the chief more to drink too, he's even crankier than Layla!" Tero's booming laughter nearly deafened Layla. He was grinning so broadly his elongated canines were showing. Layla found herself laughing along with him. It was said there was nothing more contagious than a Torski's laughter.

Then again, Tero was only half-Torski, a thought that often made her wonder just how brave a woman his mother must have been. Even with his human blood, Tero was over six and a half feet tall and claimed to be over three hundred pounds. The Torski were heavy-gravity worlders, powerfully muscled and built like a brick wall. By all reports, they were big *all* over. Not that she'd ever get a chance to find out...

The chief had made it very clear when she'd signed on to his crew that while he had no problem having a woman onboard, he'd dump her ass at the first resupply station they came across if she started any trouble between the men.

"No bed-hopping," Mace had crossed his thick arms across his massive chest and scowled at her from across the desk, his entire focus on her in a way that made her feel about three inches tall.

"If you want to sleep with one of my guys, go for it, but that's it, just one. You make your choice and then you to stick by your choice for the rest of the tour. I don't need my guys tearing themselves apart over a woman again." Mace had never said another word about it, but Layla remembered the rules and lived by them. She just wished she had known she'd never be able to choose between them.

They were a five-man crew, and her four crewmates were all of the panty-meltingly hot variety. Six months later, she still couldn't choose, which had resulted in the longest sexual dry spell of her adult life.

Asteroid mining paid well, sure. It had to. Otherwise, no one would risk their neck out here. It was dangerous, tedious work, and being stuck in the ass end of the known galaxy on a one-year contract meant she'd discovered new levels of boredom. By the time they got back to civilization, or at least what passed for it this far out, she was going to be horny enough to jump a Jeskyran, body thorns and all.

"Drink up," Jax told her as he nudged her now-refilled mug toward her hand. "This is a new batch. I think you'll find it more to your liking. I sweetened the mix a fraction and added something special." The big blond engineer winked at her.

He was all about the details, and as she cautiously sipped his newest creation, she caught herself wondering if he was as detail oriented in bed as he was everywhere else. Lust ignited a fire in her blood, and for the thousandth time since coming on board the *Kessel Queen* she found herself wondering what it would be like if she didn't have to choose between them. *In my dreams, maybe. But sadly it'll only be in my dreams...*

"This is good stuff. Your best batch yet." She smacked her lips and smiled at Jax, who beamed at the praise. She tipped her head back and drained the mug. "Hit me again."

"You keep drinking like that, and G'arn is going to have to treat you for liver failure tomorrow morning," Mace grumbled and tipped his head toward the Pheran, who acted as the crew's medic.

G'arn chuckled, the variegated blue tints to his skin shifting slightly as he laughed. To Terran eyes, the Pheran race all looked a little like the long-extinct tigers of Earth. Rounded eyes and a broadened nose gave them something of a catlike face, while their talon-tipped hands and tufted, pointed ears added to the similarities. Of course, tigers weren't blue, but the resemblance was uncanny.

"She's tougher than the rest of us put together, chief. I still think she's got Pheran blood in her somewhere. Besides, we're all scheduled for three days of downtime now we've got the ship prepped for the storm headed our way. Plenty of time for all of us to recover, even the soft Terrans."

"Who you callin' soft, ya big blue kitty-cat?" Jax teased. Knowing exactly what would happen next, Layla dove out of the way. Just in time to avoid being in the line of fire. G'arn launched himself across the table at Jax, snarling curses as he hit the bigger man square in the chest.

The impact knocked both men backward and added another set of dents to the already battered walls. Claws squealed as they connected with the metal bulkhead and the sound tore across nerves already raw from boredom and cabin fever.

She made a run for the galley and managed to dodge Tero's massive fist as he took a swing at someone, but the hooch had muddled her reflexes. She didn't quite make the corner. Instead, she ended up careening into the food dispenser. Her stomach heaved and the floor dropped out from under her.

Veth, Mace must have turned off the gravity in this part of the ship. She should have expected that. It was damned near impossible to fight in zero-g and tended to put a stop to their occasional brawls. Layla found herself spinning, which was never a good thing in zero gravity, and an even worse situation when there were three other men and a minefield of crap in her flight path.

She threw out her arms and legs, trying to stabilize herself, and managed to slow down to a before everything went sideways. Or more accurately, everything went downward, as Mace reactivated the grav plates without a word of warning. Layla felt herself falling.

Landing was going to be a bitch.

"I'M REALLY SORRY, CORBIN." Mace sounded contrite, and she wished like hell there was a way she could see his face right now. But her eyes were wrapped in some sort of light-dampening bandages that were going to keep her in the dark for the next twenty-four hours or so.

The landing hadn't actually been too bad. "There is no way you could have known I'd be blinded by an errant bowl of soup when you turned the grav plates on again. I don't even want to know the odds of that happening. It has to be a billion to one."

Her head was still fuzzy from the hooch, and now it

was further muddled by whatever painblocker G'arn had given her.

"She's going to be fine, chief. The burns are already starting to respond to treatment. The bandages can come off in a day or so, and there won't be so much as a scar to mar her pretty face. She's going to be a bit loopy once the painblockers kick in, though. I want her to rest, so I gave her something with a serious punch. We'll need to get her to her bunk soon and let her sleep it off."

"Is that what it takes for a girl to get some attention paid to her around here? Burns and bruises?" Layla turned her head toward the sound of G'arn's voice. "If so, you can consider me a damsel in distress for the next while." She fluttered a hand near her cheek. "Whoever will take care of poor, helpless, meek little me?"

"Meek. Right." G'arn chuffed with laughter. "Since when? I will agree that seeing as how you're going to be blind for the next while, I think we're all going to get to take care of you. I, for one, am going to volunteer to tuck you in." She felt a tickle of warm air near her ear and had to resist the urge to turn toward it. She could just make out G'arn's warm, spicy scent over the more clinical odors of the medical bay, and he was only a few inches away from her.

"Well, she certainly sounds like she's going to be

fine," Jax spoke from somewhere off to her right, and Layla could hear regret and worry in his tone. "She is, right G'arn? Those bandages are just a precaution?"

"I'm going to be fine, Jax. And you can tell Tero to come in and see for himself. I can hear him lurking in the hallway."

"I wasn't lurking," Tero protested. "And how did you know I was even here?"

"Are you kidding? We've been living in each other's pockets for six months. I don't need to be able to see you to tell you apart. I know your scents, the way you talk, the way each of you moves. I bet I could guess who's who just by touching those sexy bods of yours."

"I'd take that bet." A talon traced down Layla's cheek below the bandage, gentle as a feather. "You can touch me any time you like."

She heard a low groan from somewhere nearby and her pussy flooded instinctively to the sound of an aroused male. Her breath hitched and it took the last of her fast-fading common sense to shake her head in denial. "Sorry, G'arn. That would be against the rules. Chief's orders." The drugs had loosened her tongue. "No touching without choosing, and I couldn't choose just one." Behind the bandages, her eyelids grew heavy and her tongue suddenly felt too big for her mouth. "What did you give me anyway? That's good stuff!"

As she drifted toward sleep she felt someone's arms

around her, lifting her up and cradling her against a broad chest. The scent of sandalwood hit her nose, and she knew it was Mace holding her. Mace, the big, bossy cyborg whose rules had kept her celibate for six long months. He was the only man on the ship who didn't want her, and the one she wanted in her bed most of all.

CHAPTER TWO

MACE TUCKED his tech officer into her bunk and brushed a hand over her chestnut curls. Her normally golden skin was still too pale for his liking, reminding him again that she'd been injured because of his actions. If there was so much as a flaw in her lovely brown eyes when those bandages came off, he'd never forgive himself.

She was the most vivacious, stubborn, beautiful woman he'd ever met, and keeping his interest in her secret had been a constant battle.

When he'd seen Layla sprawled on the floor with her hands over her eyes, her breath hissing over her teeth as she tried not to cry out in pain, the leader had lost out to the man. He'd lived through battles and witnessed the death of his batch siblings during the Resource Wars. He carried the memory of each incident like a scar. Seeing Layla hurting though, that had nearly killed him. Mace wasn't sure he could ever go back to the way things had been, not now he'd finally held her in his arms.

He started to straighten and then stopped. Her quarters were so cramped there wasn't enough headroom for his six-foot-four frame. Like all cyborgs, he was built for combat. Taller, heavier, stronger, and faster than any human. Even if he hadn't been branded with the telltale barcode on his wrist, no one would ever mistake him for a normal human.

Since he didn't fit in anywhere else, he'd made his own place in the galaxy. This ship was his home, and his crew was the family he'd created to replace the one he'd lost in the war. Not everyone had stayed on, but in the years since the Resource Wars had ended their family had grown, and so had their plans. They were so close to achieving their dreams he could taste it, but it had almost gone nova on them when Natasha had come onboard and messed with their heads, and their hearts. To protect the team, he'd ordered Layla not to bed-hop. She was free to be with any member of his crew, but only one of them. He wouldn't let a female destroy everything they'd work so hard for.

It had been so clear to him at the time. By enacting one simple rule, he could protect everyone. Only now, it looked like that order was coming back to bite him in the ass.

He rearranged her blanket and stroked her cheek. "You little *peskin*. I never considered what would happen if you couldn't choose."

He moved away from her bunk, taking care in the cramped space of her quarters. He couldn't resist a chance to look around the private space of the woman who haunted his dreams. There really wasn't much to see. *Veth*, he had more in his cabin and he always traveled light. Even more notable than the lack of personal property was the fact everything she owned was stowed away or secured military-fashion. He'd seen her records, though, and she'd never served in the Interstellar Armed Forces or been on a long-haul space mission before this one.

When his eyes fell on the single holo-pic attached to the bulkhead, he instantly understood where she'd learned to stow her gear. Three men, related, judging by their appearance, were standing around a laughing woman who could have been Layla's twin. All three men wore the uniform of the IAF, the Interstellar Armed Forces. One of the men held a little girl with Layla's curls. Mace had no doubt he was looking at a picture of Layla and her family.

It took a moment for him to see the way all three men were touching the woman possessively, and the look of love in all their faces. He touched the image and zoomed in, close enough he could spot the distinctive and identical wedding rings all three men wore. Well, well.

Layla came from a poly family. A fact not noted in her records. What *was* listed was that her father, singular, had been killed in the line of duty while Layla was barely a teenager, and her mother had died in a shuttle crash a few years ago. No mention of any other family.

There was nothing else in her quarters, and as Mace turned carefully in the cramped space, it dawned on him why Layla fitted in so seamlessly with the rest of his crew. She had no attachments outside the hull of this ship. No family or friends to keep her heart tethered to a distant planet. She'd blended in and adopted them all as her family, just as they'd done with each other over the years.

He was starting to think he'd screwed up.

He stepped into the narrow corridor and was met by three accusing pairs of eyes. Yep, apparently, they thought he'd *fraxxed* up too. *Great.*

"What the *fraxx* did she mean? Your orders, chief?" Jax looked mad enough to chew through the triple-plated hull, and his two silent companions looked even angrier.

"Quit barking at me until we get to the rec area.

She needs to rest, and you can wait two minutes to get your explanation." Without waiting for a response, Mace turned on his heel and walked away from his crewmen.

The recreation area was the only part of the crew's living quarters that could be vaguely described as spacious. The *Kessel Queen* was a working vessel, which meant almost every cubic inch of space was dedicated to its primary mission as a mining ship. Crew comforts came a very distant second.

Access hatches to the ship's sim pods took up one wall, while a small but complete gym took up more than half the remaining space. A modest gathering area with seating for the entire crew covered what little space was left, giving them a place to socialize, read, or watch a vid together during their downtimes. Not that there were many of those, but they did happen. Like now. With a solar storm coming their way, the *Kessel Queen* had taken shelter on the leeside of one of the larger asteroids in the zone.

For most of the storm, the rock they were parked on would be between them and the bulk of the cosmic radiation coming their way, and during the few hours the asteroid's slow, tumbling motion would put them in harm's way, their shields should keep them safe. It was a calculated risk, given the age of the vessel and the number of jury-rigged repairs they'd had to make.

Getting out of the storm's path completely meant losing time, money, fuel, and likely their production bonuses, too. They'd had a meeting, talked it over, and unanimously agreed to take the chance.

This way, they'd only be out of commission for three days while the storm tore through space around them, giving them all a much-needed rest. Their usual schedule required long hours, either overseeing the actual extraction process or maintaining the various machines they relied on to do the work. The storm would cost them time, but it would allow them to relax for a little while.

Mace took a seat and pointed to the remaining chairs. The moment they were seated, the questions came at him hard and from all directions.

"What was with the order, chief?" Jax demanded, his green eyes flashing with anger.

"Why would you make her choose between us?" Tero pounded a fist into his open hand with a meaty thud, and there was deep anger showing in the Torski's all-black eyes.

"I know why you did it, Mace." G'arn leaned forward and Mace noted his eyes were gleaming brilliant silver, a sure sign his medic was seriously pissed off. "What I want to know is why you didn't tell us."

The two other men turned to stare at the Pheran.

"What do you mean, you know why he did it?" Tero asked. "Mind filling the rest of us in?"

"Go ahead, tell them," Mace sat back.

"Natasha. He didn't want what happened with her to happen again." G'arn looked from Tero to Jax. "Can you blame him?"

"Yes, I can *vething* well blame him!" Tero was on his feet and stomping around in circles hard enough the floor beneath them shook slightly with each footfall. "Natasha was a psychotic slut who only managed to get on board because she forged her qualifications. We all learned our lesson and agreed to put it behind us when we threw her off the ship. We would never let a woman, or anyone else, turn us against each other again. We agreed!"

Tero slammed a foot down and spun to face Mace, his canines flashing, and his normally placid expression screwed into a mask of fury. "So why would you treat us like children and give Layla an order like that without bothering to tell us?"

Jax scowled, nodded, and jerked a thumb toward the thundering Torski. "What he said."

"You done now, Tero? Or are you going to try to put a few more dents in my floor first?" Mace asked and waited for the big man to grunt and take his seat. "When I took Corbin on as our tech, I had a talk with her, yes. I told her flat-out if she hooked up with one of the crew, she'd have to live with her choice. No bed-hopping. This is the most important run of our lives, and you all know it. If we hit our targets, we'll have enough money saved to buy this ship, give her the full refit she needs, and finally be able to work for ourselves from now on. This is what we've been working toward for years, and I wasn't willing to risk a woman screwing it up again. I thought I was protecting *all* of us."

Three sets of very pissed-off eyes looked straight at him, and Mace threw up his hands. "It's possible I *fraxxed* up. There you go, I said it."

"*Re'veth*, he admitted to a mistake," Jax drawled. "Did the world end while we were yelling?"

"Don't get used to it, it's not likely to happen again in your lifetime," Mace shot back. "Look, I thought I was doing the right thing at the time, but clearly some of us have feelings for Layla, and apparently she hasn't been with any of us because she hasn't been able to choose just one." He glanced around at his crew, every one of them a friend, brother and someone he'd known for years. "So, the question is, what the *fraxx* are we going to do about it?"

Tero usually liked to sit back and let the conversation flow around him, but not this time.

He knew exactly what he wanted to do, and how they could make this work. "I think the answer to your question is obvious. Layla doesn't want to choose, so she shouldn't have to. I'm willing to share if you guys are. It's not like we haven't done it before."

"Yeah, and look how that turned out," Mace pointed out, looking straight at him.

Fair enough.

Tero had dealt with the worst of the crap Natasha had brought into their lives. Sharing her had seemed like a good idea, but it had all gone to shit pretty quick. She'd lied through her teeth about everything, from her qualifications to her motivations for signing on. The moment they'd left civilized space behind she'd twisted everyone into knots, playing head games and spreading lies in an attempt to tear the four friends apart.

It had fast become apparent that despite their agreement, she only wanted to spend time with Mace and Jax, leaving the two aliens feeling rejected and resentful. Natasha's actions had made Tero question everything from his friendships to his attractiveness, and by the time the truth had come out, he'd had been on the verge of walking away from his friends and years of work.

"Being with Layla wouldn't be like that. We already know her too well." Tero stared at his hands for a moment. "And if we do things differently this time, I think we can make sure things work out better."

"Different how?" G'arn asked, curious enough his tufted ears perked up.

"We share her, together." Tero linked his hands and locked his thick fingers into a tight ball. "All of us in one relationship instead of trying to have four separate ones."

The others stared at him. This was going to be the sticky bit. In Torski culture, group marriage wasn't uncommon, so the concept wasn't new to him. The thought of watching Layla with the others was enough to make Tero's blood boil and his dick turn to steel, but how would the others feel about it?

"All of us?" G'arn murmured and his ears twitched slightly, a sure sign he was agitated, or excited. "That's an intoxicating idea."

"I'm not sure intoxicating is the right word for how I'd feel about having to see your naked blue ass every time I saw Layla's." Jax's blond brows furrowed into a frown.

"It wouldn't have to be every time. But it couldn't be the way it was with Natasha either. I don't know about you guys, but I care about Layla. This isn't just about sex. This is more complicated than navigating the event horizon of a blackhole while juggling plasma grenades, but I think she's worth it."

"Now we're going to sit around and talk about our feelings?" Jax groaned and shook his head. "*Veth*. I care about her, too. So, if this is the only way we can all get what we want, then I'm in. But the first one of you bastards I catch ogling my fine ass is going to get a busted nose."

G'arn snickered. "Your ass is not that fine. Trust me. I've seen it enough times to know." He dropped one shoulder in the Pheran version of a shrug. "It's not like we haven't shared rooms and showers for years. I have no issues sharing Layla if she is willing to accept this arrangement. Given what she said about not being able to choose just one of us, I suspect this is something she'd be willing to consider."

Tero turned to Mace, who looked as dangerous as the solar storm raging outside their hull. His arms were crossed over his chest, and his face was an impassive mask even by *Torski* standards. "Chief?"

The big cyborg scrubbed a hand over his shorn head and sighed. "I'll take her any way I can get her. I'm pretty sure I'm in love with the little *peskin*." He threw up his hands in frustration as the others gawked at him. "Yeah, tell me about it. Big surprise to me, too."

"It shouldn't have been." Tero leaned forward and met Mace's gaze. "It was obvious to me months ago. We all care about her, and she cares about all of us. I think we need to show her the rules have changed, and give her a demonstration of just how good this could be."

Mace smiled a predatory grin that told Tero their chief had made his decision. "I think I have an idea how to do just that."

CHAPTER THREE

WAKING up blind had been at the top of Layla's list of things to never do again, but it was quickly knocked down a few pegs after she tried to dress and tidy herself up without being able to see. When she had stubbed her toes against the bed frame for the third time, she gave up and admitted defeat. With her pride stung, she'd opened up a comm line and asked for help.

Her mood improved when her request was met with eager offers of assistance, and within two minutes there were three men at her door, all of them ready and willing to help her out.

Maybe this damsel in distress thing wasn't so bad, after all.

Her room was too small for all of them to fit, but

they figured it out between them with only a few curses, thumps, and whispered threats.

"It's me, uh - Jax. I'm coming in to help you get dressed."

"I managed the basics, but I can't seem to get this jumpsuit done up properly." She gestured the front of her outfit in frustration. "Socks are also a problem. Every time I bend over, I lose my balance."

His hands settled on her shoulders, and he gently turned her around. "Move slow and take small steps. You really don't have much room in here. I didn't realize you were so cramped."

She shrugged. "I'm a lot smaller than the rest of you. Makes sense I'd get the smallest quarters. I'm pretty sure Tero couldn't even lie down in here."

"Nope," Tero called out from the corridor. "I'd have to bend myself in half to fit in there."

"Your lack of balance is a combination of the blindfold and the lingering effects of the pain-blockers I gave you yesterday," G'arn said.

"Yeah. That stuff knocked me on my ass. I don't really remember much after we got to medical."

"What do you remember?" Jax gently closed the fastenings on her jumpsuit.

"G'arn bandaging my head and telling me not to take it off for at least a day. And all of you lurking around, making sure I was going to be okay. Which was sweet."

"We were worried." Jax took her socks from her hand. "Your bunk is one step back and one to the left. Sit down, and I'll get your socks on."

She followed Jax's directions and gingerly eased herself onto the edge of her bunk. "I feel foolish. I can't even dress myself right now."

Jax slid her socks onto her feet, tutting to himself when he saw the damage she'd done before asking for help. "Next time, call one of us. We're here for you, Layla."

"I'm not used to having anyone around to help," the confession slipped out before she could stop herself.

All three men were silent for a long time, and she could almost imagine them backing away from her. They were a tightknit crew, but the they didn't do was talk about their pasts or their feelings.

It was Tero who broke the silence. "Get used to it. We're here, and we're not going anywhere."

Jax patted her leg. "What he said. I'm going to swap places with G'arn. We're inside the storm now, and the Chief wants me to doublecheck all the systems."

"Sorry. I should be the one doing that, not you." She hated feeling so useless.

"Consider it part of my punishment. We're the

idiots who got you hurt. The least we can do is help out for one day."

"Thank you," she said. There was a shuffle of feet, a few whispered words, and then someone touched her shoulder. "My turn to take care of you. If you get to your feet, I'll lead you to the sanitation chamber. I imagine you'd like to clean your teeth and comb your hair?"

"That would be great. Thanks, G'arn."

He took her hands in his and guided her into the chamber. He was the next smallest member of the crew, which was the only reason the two of them fit into the cramped space.

"Your toothbrush." He handed her the familiar object. She didn't need her sight to be able to clean her teeth at least, and by the time she was done, G'arn had managed to comb most of the tangles out of her hair. At least, the parts he could reach.

"Better?" he asked as he smoothed her hair with his hands.

"Much better." She did feel more herself, and having the three of them take care of her was wonderful, but being this close to them, touching them... it was a mocking reminder of what she really wanted but could never have. The only one missing was Mace, but she could hardly expect the big cyborg leader to dote on her.

"Then let's get you to the med-bay so I can check you over."

"Who gets the job of guiding the blind woman across the ship?"

"Getting you there is my job, but you won't be walking," Tero called out.

"I can walk. I'm blind, not broken. I just need my shoes."

G'arn took her hand and guided her forward. "Come with me, then."

She followed, expecting to be told to sit down on the bunk while someone got her shoes. Instead, he kept coaxing her along, and then another, much bigger hand claimed hers.

"Let me do this for you, please?" Tero's deep voice was softer than she'd ever heard it.

She didn't stand a snowball's chance in a supernova of saying no. "Okay. But don't you dare drop me."

"Never." Tero carried her back down to the medical bay cradled in his powerful arms, and Layla gave herself permission to enjoy every second. She laughed and rested her head on his shoulder, kicking her feet as they walked. His massive frame dwarfed her petite physique, and she knew it must look to the others like he was carrying around a doll and not a living person.

It wasn't until he set her down on the medi-bed and moved away from her that it struck Layla—in the last twenty-four hours she'd been touched more than she had in months. Physical contact was something she'd gotten used to going without, but now... now she was feeling the lack.

"Everyone out. I'll give you all an update as soon as I've done my examination."

"Bye-bye boys! Thank you." She waved in what she hoped was the right direction. Within a few seconds, the door closed, and the med-bay got quiet. She was alone with G'arn.

"I'm going to run some scans to check on your progress. You might feel a slight warming sensation, but that's all."

"Don't you need to take the bandages off?"

"Not for this. I don't want you to strain your eyes or be tempted to peek."

Tempted. He had no idea how tempted she was, and it wasn't just to open her eyes. "How long will this take?"

"Not long at all. All you need to do is hold still."

She hummed to herself as G'arn ran the scans. A brief warming of the face, a low buzzing noise that moved around her head, and it was done.

"So? What's the verdict?" She tried to keep her tone light, but she couldn't completely hide her anxiety.

"You're healing nicely, but I think we should leave the bandages on for one more day, just to be safe,"

G'arn finally pronounced his judgment and Layla sighed in relief. "So, I'm really not going to be blind?"

"No. I told you that yesterday. Don't you remember?"

"Everything after the accident is fuzzy. If you told me, I don't remember it."

G'arn exhaled sharply. "*Re'veth*. I'm sorry. I didn't realize. The damage was minor and the healing accelerant I gave you is doing its job. The bandages and rest are to make sure you heal as quickly as possible. I don't want to take any chances with your vision. And I need to check the label on the pain-blocker I gave you. I didn't realize it would affect you so strongly."

"It did the job. And now I know for sure it's going to be okay, I can endure another day with the bandages on. It's going to suck, though. I can't even dress or feed myself. How am I going to eat if I can't see what's on my plate? I'm useless at the moment, and I don't like it at all."

"Yesterday you were all for being the damsel in distress. What changed?"

"The drugs wore off," Layla retorted sharply, frustration getting the better of her. "I'm sorry. This is hard for me." She held out a hand in front of her, reaching out for him.

Warm fingers closed around hers, and she startled

as G'arn wrapped an arm around her shoulders and drew her gently against him. "Your eyes need more time to heal. Let us take care of you, Layla. Mace isn't the only one who feels guilty about what happened. If Jax hadn't goaded me or if I hadn't gone after him, you wouldn't be hurt right now. Even Tero is feeling bad because he nearly clocked you as you went darting past him. We want to make amends for our mistakes."

"I'm not good at being helpless, or useless. If you keep my eyes covered, I'm not even going to be able to watch vids. What am I going to do all day?"

G'arn chuckled and something in the sound chased a dark thrill down her spine. "Oh, we have a few ideas on how to help you pass the time, not to worry. "He stroked his clawed fingers through her hair in a tender gesture that made her want to lean into his touch again. "We'll address the eating problem before we leave the medical bay. I have food tabs I can give you. Not as tasty as real food, but you won't end up wearing it either."

"That would be great. Thanks."

"If you promise to keep your eyes closed, I will agree to remove the bandages long enough for you to have a proper shower. But you must swear to me you won't open your eyes."

The offer of a shower had Layla's complete attention. "If promising to keep my eyes closed will get me into a nice, hot shower, you have my word I won't so much as crack an eye open. And you better not peek either."

G'arn sighed as though she'd made the most unreasonable request in the world. "I had rather hoped you were going to ask me to wash your back for you."

"A lovely offer, but one I'm afraid I have to refuse." Layla felt a strong pang of regret as she lifted her head from G'arn's chest and pulled out of his embrace.

"Because of what the chief told you when you signed on, or because you don't think of me that way?"

G'arn's question stunned Layla to silence for a long time while she searched her scrambled memories of yesterday. "The chief? Who said anything about the chief?"

"You did. Yesterday. You said you couldn't choose between us." He squeezed her hand gently. "I want to know—if Mace hadn't given you that order, if there were no rules, would your answer still be no?"

"Is this purely a hypothetical question?" she asked, her heart tripping faster in her chest as she considered her answer.

"Purely."

"In that case..." She took a deep breath and threw caution to the wind. The drugs had already revealed her feelings, there was no point in hiding it anymore.

For better or worse, the truth was out there. "If there were no rules, you and I would already be in that shower, and you could wash any part of me you wanted."

An almost imperceptible tremor passed through his body and she heard his breath catch for a moment. "Thank you for being honest with me." He brushed a featherlight kiss to her forehead and then slowly released her from his arms. "Let's get you showered, and then I will re-bandage your eyes. By then, I am sure the others will be eager to see you again and hear how you are recovering."

If the chief heard her drugged ramblings, then he was probably less worried about her recovery and more focused on getting her off his ship. Still, there was nothing she could do about it now. The *peskin* was out of the bag. At least G'arn didn't seem upset about her confession. In fact, he seemed pleased. She wasn't sure what that meant, and she wouldn't until she saw Mace again. Until then, she might as well set it aside and enjoy her shower.

She nodded. "Let's do this. I'll be much better after I've showered. I can't wait to shampoo this *vething* soup out of my hair."

Since he had never actually promised not to peek, G'arn felt almost no guilt as he enjoyed the partially distorted sight of Layla's naked body beyond the translucent glass of the shower. Her body was as slender as a Pheran female's, though her golden skin and curly brown hair made her far more exotic and beautiful than he had ever found any member of his own species. She was far more outspoken too, a trait he found endlessly fascinating. He could watch her interact with the others for hours, simply enjoying her quick wit and energy.

He had always enjoyed sexual encounters with Terran females. Even Natasha had her charms in the beginning, before she showed her true colors, but Layla called to him on a deeper level. Just as he had chosen to tie his fate to the other members of the *Kessel Queen*'s crew, he knew that, given the chance, he would tie his life to Layla's. She might not be the same species, but his soul recognized her potential. She was his *vardi*, his life mate. At least, she could be, if the fates allowed it.

As she reached up to lather the richly scented shampoo into her hair, G'arn felt his cock harden until it was straining against the crotch of his pants. She was temptation made flesh for him, and he let himself indulge in a brief fantasy where he stripped and joined her in the small space, rubbing himself over her wet flesh until his scent was embedded in her skin and any male of his species would know she had been claimed.

He caught himself short as a low vibration rolled up from his chest, and he had to turn away. No woman had ever made him *kyrnn* before. Not even in the heights of passion had he been moved to make the mating sounds Terrans referred to as purring. If the others heard him, he'd never hear the end of it.

It was said that when a Pheran male found a woman who could make him *kyrnn*, he should never let her go. He intended to stay true to the saying, if Layla agreed to what they were about to propose.

When the shower shut off, he kept himself busy at the far side of the room, making enough noise she would know where he was as she dried off and then stepped carefully out of the shower. She had kept her word—her eyes were still closed and the towel he'd left for her was wrapped around her body, leaving her shoulders and legs bare. A searing jolt of desire raged through him at the sight of her, and it was all he could do to stay where he was and not tear the towel away so he could see all of her for the first time.

"G'arn? I know this is a lot to ask, but I just realized I don't know where I left my clothes. Can you help me get dressed?"

Veth, the female was going to be the death of him. Thankful she couldn't see the tell-tale bulge in his pants, he crossed the small room and touched her hand, letting her know he was there.

"Your clothes are right here." He drew her hand to where he had hung up her jumpsuit. "Let me know when you're ready for me to help you with the fastenings." When he'd laid out her things, he'd noticed the lack of undergarments. He'd spend the rest of the day thinking about the fact she was naked beneath the form-fitting garment. Well, hopefully not the rest of the day. If they had their way, she wouldn't be wearing anything at all, very soon.

As that thought made his dick turn as hard as the rocks they mined, he stepped away and left Layla to dress in privacy. The sooner she got dressed, the sooner they could get her down to the rec area and put Mace' plan into action. One way or another, this was going to be the day everything changed for the crew of the *Kessel Queen.*

――――

CHAPTER FOUR

――――

JAX WON the coin toss to see who got to carry her next, and so Layla found herself nestled in his arms as he carried her to the rec room.

"They guys have been organizing up some entertainment for you while I was checking the systems."

"How's the ship handling the storm?"

"Some minor power fluctuations. Nothing serious. We're still on the outer edge of this thing, though."

She nodded. "I know. It's going to get worse before it gets better."

Jax settled her against his chest and bowed his head to whisper in her ear. "You worry about getting better. The rest of us will deal with the storm."

They walked a little while longer in silence, and a thought struck her. At this rate, she would be really unhappy when the bandages came off and she'd be responsible for her own transportation again. She hadn't walked more than a few steps since getting hurt, and getting carried from place to place by her sexy crewmates wasn't exactly a hardship. The thought made her snicker softly, and Jax slowed his pace.

"What's so funny?" he asked.

"Oh, I was thinking that a girl could get used to getting carried everywhere. I haven't spent so much time in a man's arms since...well... before I came on board."

"And do you miss that?" Jax's voice was deeper now.

Fraxx, if Mace heard her flirting with the crew, he'd have her ass for sure, and not in a fun way. Instead of answering Jax's question, she deflected. "Well, I've never been carried around like this before, so I can't say I missed it. Ask me again after G'arn has taken the bandages off and I'm back to being self-propelled."

"You didn't answer my question," he pointed out. "Did you miss being held? Being touched? Is there someone back home you're waiting to see again?"

Well this was new, and more than a little strange. The guys almost never asked personal questions, but she saw no real harm in answering. This was talking, not flirting...right? "There's no one back home. There's no one waiting for me anywhere, to be honest. My parents are all dead, and there's no one else the universe who knows me well enough to even miss me." She made it sound so matter-of-fact, but the truth was she felt lost and lonely since her mother's death. The men on this ship were the only friends she had in the galaxy.

"*We* know you that well," Jax murmured. "You're more than just a crewmate, you're family. You know that, right?"

Her heart beat a little faster, and she let her head drop to rest on his shoulder as raw emotions surged through her veins. "You guys have been together for years. I didn't really expect..."

"We know a good thing when it comes into our lives." Jax surprised her with a gentle hug. "We all got burned once, a few years ago, so it takes us a little longer than it should to trust someone new."

"Natasha?"

"Natasha," Jax confirmed. "How did you even know her name?"

"You guys talk more than a bunch of old women," Layla teased. "Her name has come up before. Eventually, I put enough together to know she was a problem."

"Natasha very nearly tore us apart. She wanted our money and sexual attention, but not from everyone. She lied to all of us, played head games with Tero and G'arn, and nearly set Mace and me at odds more than once. If we hadn't been so close, she might have gotten away with it. It was Tero who finally got the four of us together and made us clear the air. After that, we swore we wouldn't let anyone screw us up like that again."

"And then I came along."

"Well, there were a few other technicians before we found you. Most of them were a waste of oxygen. One got so spacesick we had to call a med-evac shuttle, and we lost Jarret when the ship's life support failed for the lower decks. He panicked and forgot protocol."

Jax's voice buzzed near her ear. "And then you came along, and we slowly realized you were a perfect fit. I'm sorry you were alone in the world. I know how that feels. I'm not sorry your situation led you here, to us, though. Not many women could find a way to co-exist with four stubborn-ass men."

"I learned a few tricks from my mother," she confessed.

"She had a lot of brothers?"

"She had three husbands." Layla waited for the usual reaction. At least she wouldn't be able to see the judgment in Jax's eyes.

"So, you had three dads? How the hell did you ever manage to get away with anything?"

Well, that wasn't the question she'd been expecting. "I was very, very careful." She answered with a tiny smile. "And mostly, I got busted anyway. At least until they were killed."

"All of them?" Jax hugged her again and this time she wrapped her arms around his neck and held on tight.

"All of them." Those three little words encompassed so much pain. "Their entire squadron was lost and the IAF records are sealed, so I don't even know what really happened. One day they were sending vids, promising to be home soon, and the next, Mom and I were standing in front of three sealed coffins at their funeral."

Tears stung her sensitive eyes and she tried to blink them away, grateful Jax couldn't see them. "A few years back, Mom was killed in a shuttle accident and I woke up one day not long after and realized I had no ties to anyone on the entire planet. That's how I ended up here. I figured if I was going to spend my life lonely, I should at least get paid well for my time."

"You're not alone anymore."

Jax's whispered words almost brought her to tears again, so she reacted the only way she knew how. She pushed her pain back down deep and made a joke. "Of course I'm not alone. I haven't been alone since I got on board. I have you four lugs to keep me company and cheat me out of my bonus pay every time you talk me into a game of cards."

"We don't cheat," he informed her. "By the way, we're here."

"She's still claiming we cheat instead of accepting the fact she's a lousy card player?" Tero asked.

"There's nothing wrong with my hearing, Tero. You're going to pay for insulting my gaming skills once I can see to smack you."

"Don't even think about it!" Mace grumped from somewhere to her right. "After you conked out, it took me two damned hours to do all the paperwork and file an explanation as to how my tech ended up blinded by a flying bowl of soup during a brawl. The only reason everyone here isn't sucking vacuum is because I'm just as much to blame as the rest of you."

"I know we've all said it already, but we're sorry you got hurt, little one." G'arn's voice sounded from nearby, and she reached out toward it.

"I know you're sorry, and I want you to know I've decided who is to blame for my condition." Layla waited for a heartbeat before continuing. "I'm blaming the *re'vething* food dispenser! As soon as I can see again, I'm reprogramming it with a very large hammer."

"Only if you can cook, technician Corbin. Otherwise, you will do no such thing."

"You never let me do anything fun, Chief," she grumbled and kicked her legs like a little girl. "Hey, Jax.

You can put me down now, and then one of you can explain to me how you plan on entertaining the blind crewmate. Just please, don't let it be a sing-along."

"What, and have to listen to your caterwauling? Not a chance," Jax set her down onto some sort of lounge.

"Hey guys, is this an acceleration couch? It feels like one, but what's the special occasion?" She wriggled into the luxurious softness with a happy sigh. "Not that I'm complaining, but it's my eyes that are the problem, not the rest of me."

"Well, we wanted you to be comfortable, so I authorized the use of one." Mace' was much closer now and she heard someone move off to her left. "Don't get used to it, though, it's going back into storage the minute those bandages come off and you're cleared for duty."

"I'll enjoy it while I can, then. G'arn says the bandages can come off tomorrow. So, what's the plan?"

There was more shuffling, and someone touched her shoulder. "Before we get to the entertainment part of the program, there's a question we want to ask you." Jax's voice sounded very close and she turned her head toward the sound.

"What? What I take on my pizza? You are making pizza, right? It's my favorite."

"This is serious, Layla. Yesterday you said you couldn't choose—" Layla's pulse jumped, and she raised her hand to stop Jax before he said something that sent Mace into orbit.

"Whoa. You *all* heard me? That part of my day is a little fuzzy. Actually, it's mostly fuzzy with blurry bits. Whatever G'arn gave me knocked me on my ass."

"It's all right, Layla," Mace' voice came from down near her feet. *Fraxx*, had he just used her first name? This was getting weirder by the minute. "They heard what you said, and I explained the orders I gave you." There was a long pause. "That's what we want to talk about."

"What's there to talk about? You were very clear, Chief, and I did what you told me to. So why do I feel like I'm on trial here?"

The hand on her shoulder stroked down her arm and back up again in a soothing rhythm. "You're not on trial," Jax spoke again and she realized he was the one touching her. "We just—uh—we want to know—"

"*Veth!*" Tero rumbled and she felt the floor shake as he started stomping around somewhere to her right. She didn't need her eyes to tell her he was pacing, and likely running his thick fingers through his long, jet-black hair, messing up the braid he normally wore. "We really do suck at this, don't we? What we want to know, little one, is if the chief's order didn't exist, are there any of us you *wouldn't* want to be with?"

What the hell were they up to? "Uh, Chief? The order still stands, doesn't it? So, what does it matter?"

"It matters because I'm rescinding that particular order."

"Now? You're rescinding your order right now when I'm blind, and you're all here listening? Have you lost your *fraxxing* mind, sir?" She tried to sit up, only to feel a strong hand splay across her chest, holding her gently back against the couch.

"Let me up this *vething* minute or so help me..."

"Let her up, Tero." Mace's normally gruff voice was soft, and she felt a hand touch her ankle, not moving, just keeping a light pressure against her skin.

"I was afraid you'd hurt yourself, little one. You can't see, and you looked like you were going to try and storm off anyway."

"Well, I might have been thinking about it." Layla conceded the point. "G'arn, did you know about this?"

"Yes, *vardi*. I did."

"So when you asked me earlier..." Layla trailed off and she heard G'arn clear his throat.

"I was perhaps jumping the gun a little bit."

"You asked her already? You blue bastard!" Jax snapped, and Layla threw up her hand again.

"Boys, stop it. That's how I ended up with a face full of soup in the first place, remember? You guys asked me a question, and now I think I understand what you're asking. G'arn did a hell of a lot better job of it than the rest of you." She blew out a breath. "I couldn't choose one of you because I care about *all* of you. "

"But do you *want* all of us, little one?" Tero asked.

Oh, hell. They weren't going to let her off without a full confession. Fine then, she'd give them one. "Yes, I want all of you. I've been dreaming about that since I signed onto this crazy crew. I've fantasized about it every night. What it would feel like to have you all inside me, fucking me, making me scream your names. I even researched Pheran and Torski biology, which was insane because I knew I'd never choose between you, which meant I'd never get to use what I learned. So, yeah, I want all of you. All *four* of you, including Mace. If we're playing all our cards, there are mine. Time to put up or shut up, guys."

All four men went silent and she waited, wishing she could see the expressions on their faces.

The hand on her ankle vanished and Layla knew Mace had withdrawn. Just like he always did.

She was trying to figure out how to get back to her bunk on her own when a hand cupped her cheek.

Her pulse skittered up several notches and then took off at a gallop when Mace's voice whispered near her ear. "I want you too, Layla. So I am hoping none of us are going anywhere, not for a very long time."

"Oh." The single word escaped her lips on a sigh,

and she turned toward the sound of his voice. "You might have mentioned that earlier, sir."

"Now is not the time for calling me sir, and believe me, the guys have already called me out for my earlier decision. There's no need for you to chime in, too." His mouth brushed over hers and a shiver passed through her right down to her toes. "I believe you said something yesterday about betting you would be able to tell us apart by touch. Care to try and prove it?"

"I did?"

"Yes, you did." Mace was still close enough his breath fanned her face when he spoke.

"I can do that." Layla lifted her head and kissed him, pleased at the way his breath caught as she took control from him and ran with it. She parted her lips just enough to run the tip of her tongue across his lower lip and then dropped her head back down to the mattress. "I'm going to guess I kissed Mace. What do I win?"

"You are a difficult little *peskin*. I was just the warm-up. If you want to play for real stakes, you need to start over again." Mace kissed her cheek and then moved away.

"So, I'm literally betting blind here?" She sat up slowly. "What are the stakes?"

"We'll all kiss you. If you can guess who it is, then

you can ask them for one favor. Anything you want," Jax explained.

"And if I mess up? I sense some fine print in this deal."

"If you guess wrong, then anyone you didn't guess correctly gets to ask one favor, of *their* choosing."

Her pussy was drenched as she let her imagination run wild. It seemed the guys were done with waiting, because as far as Layla could see, there was only one way this was going to go. She was finally going to get her wish.

"You're on. And when all four of you owe me favors, I know exactly what I'm going to ask for." She caught a low rumble of arousal from one of the men and grinned. She was going to enjoy this.

"One more thing, brat. No hands," Mace instructed and she stuck out her tongue in the general direction of his voice.

"Changing the rules already, Chief? Afraid I'll grope my way to victory?" A wicked thought flashed to mind and she decided today was the day she'd see how many of her fantasies she could bring to life, starting with this one. "If you don't trust me, you could strap me down. Just my hands, mind you."

"Fuck, yes." Layla's nipples beaded in response to the need in Jax's voice. "I vote we take her up on that, Chief."

"Jax! I had no idea, big boy."

Fingers brushed her wrist, and she felt one of the safety straps crossing her body a hand's breadth below her breasts, just enough to keep her arms trapped at her sides. A buckle clicked into place, and then the strap was tightened so there was no wriggle room. "Comfy?"

"Very, thank you, Tero."

"That's it, guys, no more talking. She's disturbingly good at this, so let's not help her," Mace said, and the room went silent.

Layla tried to calm her racing pulse and pull her focus away from the needy throbbing of her pussy. This was one game she had no intention of losing.

CHAPTER FIVE

THE SENSES she had left were ramped up to eleven, and Layla was almost quivering with anticipation as she heard one of them move closer. They moved quietly, and only the soft noise of fabrics rubbing together gave them away. Soft lips brushed the corner of her mouth, and she could have sworn sparks arced between them to sizzle against her skin.

With almost painful slowness he sampled her lips, teasing and nibbling before finally kissing her fully, and the effect made her toes curl and her mouth fall open with a soft moan. A whisper of a familiar scent touched her nose and blended with the spicy flavor of his mouth, and in that instant, Layla knew it was G'arn who was kissing her with a finesse she would never have imagined.

The Pheran took his time, and when their lips

finally parted, she could barely think past the fog of lust his kiss had induced. If he was as thorough a lover as he was a kisser, she was going to really enjoy calling in his favor.

"G'arn, you can kiss me like that any time you like," she said and the Pheran chuckled in response.

"Damn it, she's *really* good at this," Jax muttered and then went silent.

"I've had six months' worth of fantasies to go on, guys. There is no way you're going to fool me."

There was a collective hiss as several of her crewmates reacted to her comment and then G'arn asked, "I'd like to hear about these fantasies of yours, *vardi*."

Instead of answering, Layla deflected. "I'll tell you about my fantasies once you tell me what *vardi* means."

"It is a term of endearment, like sweetheart," G'arn replied.

And that was what she really wanted. Sex with all of them would be amazing, but she was greedy. She wanted more than that. She wanted everything. "Is that really how you think of me? As your sweetheart?"

It was Mace who understood what she was really asking. "It is, if you want it to be."

"All of you?" She hated that she couldn't see their

faces right now. She had no way to judge their reactions.

"All of us," Tero spoke next, and the rest voiced their agreement with so much enthusiasm she felt a wave of relief.

"If you think this is going to be a one-time thing, then you can think again. We're doing this to show you that you don't have to choose," Mace said.

Her heart did a slow somersault as she absorbed what they were telling her. "So, this is how things are now? All of us? Some of us? How is this going to work?"

"Honestly? It'll probably be rough in patches," Jax said. "This isn't something we've ever done before, at least not like this."

"Sometimes we'll be together, and other times we'll want to spend time with you alone," G'arn added.

"We're going to have to work it out as we go, and no doubt we're going to have to talk about our damned feelings more than any of us would like, but we'll figure it out. The only rule is that there won't be any secrets. We're in this together."

"Together," she agreed happily. "You have no idea how much I've wanted this."

"You can tell us about that later," Mace said.

"And then you can share more about these fantasies of yours," G'arn said.

She was still trying to process everything when another set of lips met hers and banished every idea from her head. This kiss wasn't artful or gentle, it was a full-on possession. A hand cradled the back of her head as the kiss went deeper and deeper still. Passion spiked and heat seared her from the inside out as she returned the kiss in kind.

Tongues tangled as she felt her hair being tugged lightly, sending a sizzling surge of pleasure-pain straight to her swollen clit. She moaned and tried to lift an arm, then grunted in frustration as she remembered she'd suggested they restrain her. She didn't want to be restrained any more. She wanted to grab and taste and grind herself against Mace.

She wasn't even sure how she knew, but once his name came to mind she was certain he was the one turning her inside out. She'd always wondered if there was a passionate beast chained up inside the gruff, no-nonsense cyborg, and now she had her answer. There was, and he was letting the beast off its chain, just for her. This was the one man she didn't think would ever want her, but with his hands in her hair and his lips ravaging hers, there could be no doubt he did.

She had to bite back a whimper of disappointment when the kiss finally ended. She hadn't wanted to stop. Hell, she'd even forgotten about their audience, but by the sounds of ragged breathing, they had all been paying rapt attention to her. She licked her lips, savoring the taste of him. "If I had known you could kiss like that, I would never have agreed to your order, sir."

"Don't call me sir, brat." She could hear the raw passion roughening his voice and she knew she'd guessed right. "How'd you know?"

"What, and give away my secrets while the game is still in play? Not a chance. Besides, a girl needs a little mystery. It adds to our allure."

"You've been secretly fantasizing about us for months. I think you've already exceeded your secrets limit," G'arn muttered and Layla found herself actually giggling at the reproach in his tone.

A featherlight touch to her cheek drew her attention back to the moment, and she turned her head to nuzzle the finger touching her. Warm and incredibly gentle, the solitary finger drew down her cheek to her throat and her breath caught as the touch continued down to the first fastening of her jumpsuit, slowly easing it open, followed by the next, and the next.

"I should have thought of that," Mace grumbled.

Before she could comment, her mystery lover was baring her chest to the cooler air of the rec area. Her nipples tightened instantly, both from the temperature change and the idea that four horny men were currently staring at her breasts and she couldn't cover herself or stop them.

The gentle touch returned, tracing a line down the valley dividing her modest breasts, and her heart pounded against her ribs hard enough he had to be able to feel it, too.

A rustle of fabric was the only warning she got before hot breath fanned over her breast and her nipple was engulfed in wet heat. Her pussy creamed and she cried out in wordless need as a tongue swirled around her diamond-hard nub. The scalding heat of his mouth was her first clue.

Torski biology ran hotter than human, and that gave him away. A sharp point dragged across her tender flesh, making her blood sing. Thick fingers teased and rolled her other breast, and she threw back her head to cry out, basking in the heat of Tero's touch. Her mind raced as she imagined what it would feel like to have the hot length of his cock inside her. The thought had her channel walls flexing with the aching need to have something to fill her pussy.

"Tero, you're killing me." She moaned and then mewled again as he nipped her harder, not bothering to hide his fangs any longer. One massive hand cupped her cheek and he released her breast with an audible pop.

"Now you have guessed, may I have a kiss?" His

voice was so thick with desire his speech was more rumble than words.

"Baby, you can have anything you want," she told him and then moaned into his mouth as it sealed over hers. She was surprised to discover he tasted like cloves. She swept her tongue deeper into his mouth and he groaned loud enough the vibration passed right through her. His massive hand covered one breast again and she could feel the pebbled nipple jut against the warmth of his palm.

"Tero, ease up. She already guessed it was you." Mace's voice was tinged with laughter. And her heart swelled with joy when she realized that laughter was all she heard. There was not a drop of jealousy or anger in Mace's tone.

Tero only growled in response and kissed her harder, and Layla was amazed at the depths of need she could sense in her normally stalwart crewmate. All of them had been hiding so much from each other for the past six months, and now things were racing to what promised to be one hell of an explosive climax.

When her lungs were burning with the need for air, she nipped at Tero's lips and turned her head to end their kiss, and he finally lifted his head so she could breathe. His fingers stroked her cheek before withdrawing, and then she was alone in the darkness again.

She didn't like the feeling.

"I think there's a flaw in this plan of yours, guys. I know Jax is the only one left, so I win by default, but that's not exactly fair."

"*Re'veth,* she's right."

"Come over here and untie me, Jax. I think I have a way to make it up to you." She deliberately arched her body against the single strap holding her in place and grinned as she heard footsteps head her way almost at a run. The strap came off within seconds and she reached for him, needing his touch. He wrapped her in his arms and drew her against his chest, tucking her head under his chin as he just held her a moment.

"Finally," he breathed the word so softly she knew no one else could have heard, and then spoke loudly enough everyone could hear. "So, how are you going to make this right?"

She slid her arms around his broad chest and rubbed herself up against him like a cat. "I want to— no, I *need* to come. I think you should be the one who gets me off. Please?"

"I think that's the best idea I've ever heard." His arms tightened around her, and she moved her head out from under his chin. The moment she did, he dropped his head to kiss her, taking her breath away when his lips slanted over hers. Unadulterated need flavored his kiss, and she gave him everything he demanded and more besides.

NOTHING COULD HAVE PREPARED Jax for the exquisite torture of watching the woman he craved share herself with the men he considered his brothers. It was hotter than he could have imagined, and jealousy had only reared its ugly head when he realized she'd been able to guess everyone else's identity, ending their little game before he'd had a chance to taste her for himself.

When she'd made her suggestion, envy had turned to lust in a second, and every minute he'd spent watching was suddenly worth the wait. Layla's hot little body was finally in his arms, and her mouth was as sweet and welcoming as he'd imagined it would be. He wanted to be inside her so badly he ached, and it was all he could do to keep from tearing her clothes off and fucking her right then and there.

He broke off their kiss with a reluctant groan, lifting his head just enough to be able to see her as he undid her jumpsuit the rest of the way and slid a hand down her body from pert breast to her bare pussy. "You're not wearing underwear." He traced the seam of her labia with one finger. "I need to taste this, Layla. I need to eat this sweet, bare pussy until you come. Is that what you want me to do?”

A shuddering moan gave him his answer, and he could swear the sound went straight to his dick, making it harder than it had ever been before.

“Mouth, fingers, tongue, cock, I don't care, Jax. Just please make me come. I need to so bad it hurts right now.”

“It won't hurt for long, sweetheart. I'm going to make you feel so good, and then I think the others want to do the same.”

“That's what I want, too.” She wriggled her hips so her pussy ground against his hand. “So why am I still dressed?”

“Because you have to let go of me before I can get this off of you, smart-ass.” He flicked at the swollen hood of flesh over her clitoris, making her gasp. She untangled her arms from around his chest to shed the jumpsuit on her own. The minute she had her arms free, he lifted her out of it so the garment slid off her legs to the floor. She was finally, gloriously naked.

Fraxx, she was perfect. Delicate curves, soft skin, and slender limbs made to wrap around a man and welcome him home. As she kicked herself clear of the last of her clothes, he lifted her back onto the acceleration couch, so her legs dangled over the side.

“Someone get behind her, so she's got something to

hang onto." He didn't wait for them to move. He simply sank to his knees and placed his hands on her inner thighs, coaxing her to open her legs wider so his shoulders fit between her knees. She did him one better, lifting her legs one at a time and settling them on his shoulders, her ankles crossed so they were locked together.

She reached down and found his head after a moment of blind exploration, and gripped his hair tight before pulling his face closer to her pussy. Her meaning was clear, and Jax was more than happy to oblige her silent command. He pressed his face against her slick lips and groaned as the heady scent of her cream filled his senses. This was heaven, or as close to it as a man like him was ever likely to get.

CHAPTER SIX

JAX'S HEAD was between her thighs, his tongue lapping at her throbbing clit, finally offering her relief from the sexual firestorm raging inside her. When another set of arms curved around her, Layla sank back into them, releasing Jax's hair so she could rest her back against a warm chest. A warm, *bare* chest.

"You look so lovely right now, *vardi*." G'arn's voice flowed over her skin like silk. "Your skin is flushed, and these..." He stroked the tips of his claws over her breasts, the sharp points gliding across her skin. "These are so beautiful."

Layla could only moan in answer as Jax zeroed in on her clit, working it with his tongue in a series of quick, sharp lashes that had her thighs tightening around his head, locking him to her body. He responded with a muffled laugh that sent a shimmer of heat up the empty walls of her channel. G'arn's claws kept up their slow dance around her sensitive nipples, teasing them into hard buds.

"He's going to make you come now, Layla. I can tell because your scent is getting stronger, and your skin looks as painted with fire, it's so flushed and heated." A sudden, exquisite bite of pain coursed through her as G'arn pinched her nipples with his claws and she cried out in shock and pleasure.

Her cries seemed to encourage Jax, who pushed two fingers into her pussy as he attacked her clitoris with mouth and tongue. Layla's cries morphed into a lingering wail of bliss as she felt her orgasm bloom and then consume her.

Her senses were still reeling as Jax gently ducked himself out from between her thighs. Strong hands took her legs and G'arn's arms were around her chest and she found herself being carried and then settled onto what felt like a bunk mattress, but there wasn't anything like that in the rec area.

She leaned first to one side and then another, but she couldn't feel anything but bedding, and she wished yet again she could see. Well, G'arn *did* owe her a favor of her choosing now...

"G'arn is there any way I can have these bandages off? I want to be able to see all of you, please?"

The Pheran huffed in thought somewhere nearby

and then sighed. "If we dimmed the lights almost completely, I suppose you could take them off. It would be better if you didn't though. Your eyes still need time—"

"Thank you!" she interrupted, fumbling for the taped end so she could get it off before he changed his mind.

"I'll get the lights," Mace said from right beside her and she felt the mattress shift as he moved away. She hadn't even realized he'd been so close. These bandages definitely needed to go. Another pair of hands closed over hers, stilling her movements.

"I'll do this, little one," Tero said and she withdrew her hands from beneath his, leaving him to unwind the bandages. He did so with such gentleness she barely felt each layer come away.

"Be sure to keep your eyes closed until I tell you to open them," G'arn reminded her.

"They're closed." She frowned as her stomach fluttered and her limbs lightened. "And who's *fraxxing* with the grav plates again? This is how I ended up blind in the first place!"

"I am." Mace's voice came from close by again. "Relax, I dialed it back to three-quarters standard, that's all."

"You could have warned me! And why turn down the gravity at all?"

"Because, you little *peskin*, I thought it might make things more fun."

Someone tweaked a lock of her hair as the last of the bandages fell away. Layla sighed in relief and ran her fingers through her hair, fluffing up the curls as she massaged her itchy scalp.

"If you don't stop calling me that, chief, we're going to be having words. I know what a *peskin* is, and I'm not flattered. "

G'arn chuckled. "You should be. They are the most beautiful things I have ever seen. You may open your eyes now, slowly."

"Yeah, with a nasty temper and a tendency to bite and scratch," she shot back and then eased her eyes open. The light was dim, but it was bright enough to see by, and the first thing she saw was Mace, his eyes full of concern. As her eyes drifted from his face to his bare chest, her libido's engines revved up again.

"Now that's a very nice image to open my eyes to." She reached out to run her fingers through the dark smattering of hair covering his chest. He knelt in front of her, shirtless but still wearing his pants. He rarely left his arms bare, and she took a moment to look at the barcode tattooed on his left wrist. It marked him as a cyborg, though she had never seen him as anything but a man.

"I'm just glad you can see," he said, the worry

fading from his eyes. "And now you can see again, I believe we're all eagerly waiting to hear what your wishes are."

Layla looked around her and grinned as she drank in the lust-inducing view. The others had gathered up every bit of bedding on board and built a bed big enough for all of them. She was settled in the middle, with the four of them kneeling in a ring around her, shirtless and staring at her with barely restrained hunger. They all wanted her just as much as she wanted them. She held their hearts in the palm of her hand, and the realization made her head spin and her pussy cream.

"My wish? It's the same one I've had since I got here. I don't want to choose between you. I'm greedy, I want all of you. And I want all of you together."

"*Re'veth*! I owe Tero a bottle of the good stuff," Jax muttered from off to her left, and Tero's booming laughter filled the air.

G'arn ran his fingers through her hair and then leaned down to kiss her bare shoulder. "I saw the picture in your quarters today, little one. You had three fathers, didn't you? Three men, all in love with the same woman. That is when I knew this was going to work."

She turned from G'arn to stare at Jax. "I can't believe you had a bet on whether or not I'd be up for taking on all four of you. If you hadn't just made me see stars, Jax, I'd smack you upside the head right now!"

"You can punish him later," Mace said and winked at her. "Right now, we're discussing what you want, and having you in front of me, gloriously naked, is making it *fraxxing* hard to think."

"Then stop thinking and get undressed." Layla was amazed her voice sounded so calm given the way she was screaming in jubilation inside her head. "I want to see what I've been missing all these months."

They all got to their feet, and she sat back to enjoy the view as they stripped. Not even in her wildest dreams had it ever been this good.

G'arn was lean compared to the others, but his body was a study in streamlined elegance, every muscle and sinew showing beneath the blue striping covering his entire body. Her eyes dropped to his erection and her mouth watered. Proportionate to the rest of him, he was slimmer in girth, but he more than made up for it in length. Jax's heavier build lacked G'arn's definition, but he was just as hot in his own way. Scruffy blond hair, unshaven chin and a treasure trail of blond hair that led her eye down to another impressive cock.

She idly wondered if there was some sort of minimal measurement required to be a member of this crew, and the image of the guys whipping their dicks out to be measured had her laughing as she turned her attention to Mace. He wasn't as long as G'arn or as large as Jax, but as she let her appreciative gaze run over his naked form, her breasts tightened, and her clit tingled in anticipation of what was going to happen next.

"Tero?" She turned her head, looking for the only one missing from the group.

He was standing behind her, still wearing his pants, though his hands rested on the fastening. She was struck by the look of uncertainty on his face and the doubt gleaming in his jet-black eyes.

"What is it?" She stood, bouncing to her feet when she forgot to accommodate the lowered gravity. She placed her hands over his, marveling at the size difference between them. Without another word, she shifted her hand lower, stroking the hard length of him through his pants.

"I want to see you," she murmured. He was silent, but she could feel the tension vibrating through him. It galled her that someone had done a number on her sweet Tero's confidence. She slid her hands into his pants and wrapped them around the thick shaft of his dick and silently vowed if she ever clapped eyes on Natasha, she'd bitch-slap her for making Tero doubt himself. She stroked all the way down to the root of his cock and was rewarded with a low groan.

"These need to come off, sexy." She tugged at his pants one-handed, unwilling to let go of his dick. That finally got him moving, and he shed the last of his clothing and stood in front of her, gloriously naked and so hot it made her pussy clench.

"I know I'm too big..." he started to speak and she tightened her grip on his cock, stopping his words.

"You are not too big. We're going to need to go slow, that's all." She lifted her gaze to grin up at him, feeling like a queen commanding her knights. Granted, a *naked* queen. "I did my research, sexy. And believe me, I'm going to enjoy the hands-on part of this learning experience." She pumped his shaft again and swiped her thumb over the head, spreading the hot pre-cum over his skin. "So, here's my first request. I want you to lie down on this lovely big bed you boys made up for us and let me ride this incredible cock."

Tero growled and then his hands were on her ass, lifting her high into the air so they were nose to nose. "I love you, Layla. I promise I won't hurt you."

"Of course you won't." She laughed and brushed a kiss to his mouth. "You're my sexy teddy bear. Now, put me down and let me get the rest of the guys organized." She dropped her voice to a silken whisper so the others wouldn't hear her heartfelt confession. "I love you, too."

"Did she just call three hundred pounds of Torski a *fraxxing* teddy bear?" Jax asked the room. "G'arn, are you sure her vision's okay?"

Tero set her down slowly, letting their bodies slide together for several tantalizing seconds before her feet touched the ground. He stroked his hand up her spine and then stepped away, looking far more confident and happier than he had been a short time ago.

"I hope one of you thought to bring barrier gel to this party," she quipped as she walked over to G'arn, relishing the way all of their eyes followed her as she moved. She brazenly fisted his cock and stood on tiptoes to kiss him in greeting. "My wish is for you to take my ass."

G'arn made a low, rumbling noise that sounded so much like a purr Layla blinked in surprise. "Is that a yes?"

"Yes, *vardi.* "

"No way. You purr?" Jax managed to get the words out between gales of laughter. "Why did I not know this?"

"Because a Pheran only *kyrnns* when they are with someone they desire greatly," Layla answered Jax without looking away from her silver-eyed lover. "I guess you aren't G'arn's type."

"You know what *kyrnning* is?" G'arn's beautiful eyes were wide with surprise.

"I do. I told you guys, I did research. *Lots* of research." She moved her hand down G'arn's cock to press a finger into a small notch just above the root of his shaft, and G'arn growled low in response. She pressed harder and he threw back his head and howled.

"*Re'veth*! Where did you learn that?" he asked when he could speak again. His skin had darkened several shades and his dick had swelled in her hand.

"Damn, she's dangerous," Tero muttered from behind her and she glanced back to see him lying on the floor, his cock in his hand as he waited for her to join him.

"I've had six months of involuntary celibacy. You have no idea how dangerous I am right now." Layla released G'arn with a wink and made her way back to Tero, straddling his massive chest and laughing when her knees didn't even reach the mattress. Tero settled his hands on her hips to help her balance and she trusted him to keep her in place. She locked eyes with Mace and crooked her finger at him.

"C'mere, Mace. I want to suck that cock of yours so I can watch as you finally let yourself lose control."

Mace's eyes gleamed like cobalt-blue lasers as he dropped to his knees at Tero's shoulder, his erection standing straight up from between his muscular thighs. "Who says I'm going to lose control?"

"I say so," she challenged him, and he leaned in close to rake his lips across hers.

"We'll see, gorgeous."

Jax stood off to one side, his green eyes full of heat as he looked down at the scene in front of him. "Got room for one more?"

"Of course," she pointed to the mattress beside her. "This is what I want. All of you." She felt a tremor pass through her as she finally realized she was truly about to get what she wanted. Her fantasies were about to become a reality. These were her males, ready to love her and be with her. Maybe, just maybe, they'd find a way to come together and create the family she had been missing.

Jax sank onto the mattress and grinned. "We're going to have to work on your communication skills, sweetheart. If you wanted this, you could have just asked."

"Well, I'm asking now."

"More like ordering," Mace grumbled and flicked a forefinger at one pert nipple. "Don't get used to it."

CHAPTER SEVEN

THERE WAS NO SIGNAL, at least none Layla saw, but somehow all four men seemed to move as one to reach for her at the same time. Four pairs of hands caressed, stroked, and fondled every part of her and she felt a heady, heated rush.

She let all the sensations blend until she was caught up in a whirlwind of need. She watched Tero squeeze a generous portion of barrier gel onto his fingers and fisted his cock, coating himself with the gel. It was the perfect protection and lubricant—a micro-thin barrier that allowed full sensation but prevented any risk of disease or pregnancy. When his hand returned to her hip, it was slick with the gel, gliding over her skin like hot silk.

Two hands worked her nipples, the touch different enough to tell her they didn't belong to the same man.

It was getting difficult to think, her overstimulated body demanding release and blocking out everything else.

Tero drew her down his broad body toward his erection and Layla leaned over, bracing herself against his shoulders as she slid her pussy over the massive length of his dick. In the lesser gravity it was easier to support herself, and she started to understand why Mace had dialed the grav settings down.

The thick head of Tero's cock was pressed against her pussy and Layla rolled her hips, driving him in a scant inch, making both of them groan. Damn, he was *big*. She rolled her hips again and sank a little farther, the burn and stretch warring with the immense pleasure building as his shaft rubbed along every nerve ending she had.

Screw it. Layla dropped her mouth to Tero's, relaxed, and let gravity pull her down on top of him. She didn't stop until she was so full of him she could barely move.

"*Veth!*" Tero snarled. "What happened to going slowly?" Before she could answer, he kissed her so hard their teeth clicked together.

She was reeling with sensual overload by the time Tero's mouth left hers, but she had played this scenario out in her fantasies. Layla lifted her head, clenching her pussy walls around Tero's cock and reached for

Mace, coaxing him close enough she could swipe the tip of her tongue over the head of his dick.

Mace's breath hitched and he tangled his fingers into her hair as he thrust lightly forward, pushing deeper into her mouth. She curled her tongue around his glans and he groaned, his fingers tightening in response.

G'arn moved in from behind and reached between her and Tero to toy with her swollen clit, tearing a moan from her throat and making her buck against the sweet pressure of his fingers. She rocked back and forth on top of Tero in a slow, careful rhythm, and each movement sent a scintillating wave of sparks and lust racing through her veins.

She moaned again, letting the vibrations travel from her mouth to Mace's cock as she lapped and sucked along his hard length. Grateful for the lesser gravity, Layla turned to reach for Jax, balancing her weight on one hand as she wrapped her fingers around his dick and stroked it in the same slow rhythm.

"This is…" Jax trailed off as she slid a finger over his balls on her next downward stroke.

"Perfect." Mace finished Jax's sentence.

"Not yet it isn't." G'arn reached between her and Tero to press against her clit, pushing her to the edge of another orgasm. Her inner walls pulsed and tensed, and she sucked harder on Mace, while her grip on Jax's cock tightened, and all three men groaned.

"Whatever you just did, don't do it again unless you want this all over before you join the party. She nearly set us all off."

G'arn growled deep in his throat and eased his hand out from between Layla's thighs, making her mewl with disappointment.

"I know, *vardi*. You are always so impatient." G'arn stroked slick fingers down the cleft of her ass. "You will wait for me, and no more complaining."

The edge to his voice made Layla's pussy pulse and her cream gushed down to coat Tero's balls. G'arn was usually quiet unless provoked. Hearing him issue her an order made her hotter than she would have believed possible. She hummed an affirmation, and Mace chuckled as the vibrations coursed through him.

"I think she just agreed, but she might just have been trying to turn my balls inside out. It's *fraxxing* hard to tell right now." Mace tugged playfully at her hair. "Nice try though."

She responded by deep-throating Mace and swallowing several times in quick succession. Mace growled something unintelligible as a tremor passed through him, and she eased back, her lips curving into a grin.

That was the moment G'arn pressed his fingers to

her anus, the barrier gel on his hand causing him to slip inside with relative ease. He worked the first digit deeper and then added another finger, coaxing the tight ring of muscle to relax. The dark burn of his touch had her vibrating with uncontrollable need, and she pressed back against his hand, her control slipping several notches in the course of a few seconds.

G'arn swiftly replaced his fingers with his cock, pressing himself gradually into her body, and both she and Tero groaned at the pleasurable invasion.

"So tight now," Tero grunted and wrapped his arms around her waist, holding her in place when she began to buck and thrust again. "Easy, little one. G'arn's right, you need to learn some patience."

She snarled in frustration, flexed her pussy around his cock, and sped up both her mouth and hand.

"Son of a starbeast—quit telling her to be patient, you two, or she's going to be the death of us all!" Jax warned.

Layla would have laughed, but she was too far gone into bliss. She was a creature of pure sensation, carnal and dark. She was the focal point of four men, all of them bound to each other through her, and the feeling was like nothing she'd ever imagined. None of her fantasies could compare to the reality of this moment. G'arn thrust so deeply his body pressed against her ass before withdrawing, and she found herself rocking back and forth in time to his thrusts. She rode both their cocks, letting G'arn dictate the pace as she gave herself over completely.

Thrust and counter, suck and stroke, they ascended together, all of them reaching for that elusive peak. It was Tero that pushed Layla over the edge. He used his gel-covered hand to slide between their bodies and rubbed his calloused fingertip over her clit. Lights shimmered at the edges of her vision, and her entire body went taut as a bowstring as her orgasm swelled and then exploded, sending her senses flying.

The sound of flesh hitting flesh and the wild groans of her lovers filled her ears as she screamed around Mace's cock, and then Tero's already hot flesh grew almost scalding as he bellowed in triumph and surged up into her. G'arn's body covered hers, his hips slamming against her as he fucked her hard and fast before muffling his cries against her shoulder as he shuddered to orgasm. Jax's cum coated her fingers as she pumped him ruthlessly, milking him dry. Only Mace managed to hold back, and Layla laughed as she took up the challenge.

Humming softly, she leaned in and took Mace's entire length into her mouth, using her tongue to stroke every inch until he was pressed against the back of her throat. Only then did she start humming louder, bobbing her head in a steady rhythm while her other men slowly recovered around her.

She heard Mace growl, and both hands cradled her head as he finally lost control. She released Jax's softening dick to cup Mace's balls and his entire shaft thickened instantly. His hips started to rock as he fucked her mouth, and Layla shifted her grip so she could stroke a finger along the sensitive skin behind his scrotum.

The moment her finger drew along that tender strip of flesh, Mace shuddered and came, pouring his seed down her throat as he panted and groaned above her. The moment he could draw breath, he mumbled her name and bowed his body over hers to plant a kiss between her shoulder blades before resting his sweat-dampened forehead on her back.

She released him from her mouth and slumped into a boneless heap on top of Tero, a rush of emotion hitting her from out of the blue. Tears stung her eyes and tracked down her face as she tried to come to terms with everything they had just shared. It had been unforgettable, and she finally allowed herself to truly acknowledge the love she had for the four men she had lived and worked with every day for the past half a year.

Tero, her gentle giant. Jax, the jokester whose rough hands could play such beautiful music on his guitar. G'arn, the quiet one who watched everything, and Mace, their leader, who kept himself distanced from everyone and never let down his guard, at least not until today. She loved them all, and for the first time, she dared to hope they all loved her, too. *Well, at the very least, they want me. That isn't a bad place to start.*

"*Fraxx*, she's crying." It was Tero who noticed first, hardly a surprise since her tears were soaking his chest. "Did I hurt you?"

G'arn withdrew and came around to join the others, dropping to his knees between Mace and Jax. "*Vardi*? What is wrong?"

"Nothing," Layla felt foolish, getting caught crying, but she could no more stop her tears than she could have ordered the planets to stop spinning. "Nothing's wrong. No one hurt me." She lifted her head and found four sets of eyes staring at her, all of them wearing matching expressions of concern.

"I'm just happy."

Jax blew out a relieved breath. "Women. What is with the fairer sex and the happy tears thing? You about gave me heart failure, sweetheart! I thought we'd done something wrong."

"No, you all did everything right. I just... I've wanted this for so long and now..." She trailed off and swiped at her tears with the back of her hand.

"You are going to make your newly healed eyes

irritated and sore," G'arn reached down and stroked her cheek, wiping away more of her tears.

Mace smiled at her. "You're not the only one who wanted this. I'm just sorry it took you getting hurt to make us do something about it. This isn't going to be easy, But I'm damned sure I'm not the only one in love with you, brat, so we'll just have to figure it out."

His words triggered another wash of tears, and G'arn muttered as he wiped her cheek again. "If you don't stop crying, then I'm going to send you back to medical. As it is, I think you're going to need another injection of healing accelerant to repair the inflammation you're causing right now." He surprised her by kissing her softly. "So, since you're going to need another trip to medical anyway, I love you, too."

"Me too, sweetheart," Jax joined in, his hand resting on her shoulder. "But please, stop crying. It's my fault you got hurt in the first place, so no more tears on my account."

"It would be a lot easier to stop crying if you guys would stop being so *vething* sweet!" she groused, but her entire being was filled with light and joy, and she knew they could see right through her complaints. "And you're all slow, too. Tero told me he loved me before he made me come, unlike you lollygaggers."

"What the *fraxx* is a lollygagger?" Jax asked.

"A better question might be, do you love us?" G'arn asked, his voice little more than a husky whisper.

"Yes." She sat up and made eye contact with each of them in turn. "Oh, yes. I love all of you. That's why I couldn't choose. How could I?"

"Well, that's settled then," G'arn huffed softly. "Now, if you would disengage yourself from Tero, I want to take a look at you back at medical."

"No." She crossed her arms over her naked chest.

"I need to see to—"

"I said no. I'm not ready for this to be over yet. My eyes will be fine, G'arn."

"Is there something else you need, little one?" Tero rumbled with amusement from his vantage point beneath her.

"Definitely. First, I need a rest, and then I think we need to do that again. Only this time, can we turn down the gravity some more?"

"She's going to be the death of us," Jax muttered.

"Maybe, but I can think of worse ways to go," Mace replied. She couldn't have agreed more.

CHAPTER EIGHT

IT WAS six long and glorious hours before G'arn finally managed to talk her into getting her eyes checked. Mace had ended the discussion by carrying her to the medical bay himself, G'arn complaining the whole way about difficult patients who thought they knew better than a trained medic.

Layla was feeling far too mellow to even bother to argue with him. She curled into Mace's arms and relaxed, every muscle aching pleasantly, and her entire body humming with contentment. They had left the others to tidy up the rec area and decide on the evening meal, which likely meant they'd be having synth steaks with all the trimmings, again.

She hadn't told them, but she was actually a very good cook. Layla just never admitted to it because she had worked her ass off to make sure they thought of her as a miner, one of the team, and not just the domestic help. Not that they had ever made her feel that way, but she'd been careful to make sure she had blended in. At least she had up until today. There was no way any of them was ever going to think of her as just one of the guys now. She lifted her head and found Mace smiling down at her. All in all, she was more than okay with that.

G'arn had given her drops to sooth the irritation her earlier tears had caused and then injected her with another dose of healing accelerant. "That's the last one you can have though, *vardi,* so try to avoid getting injured again for at least a week. Your body really can't tolerate much more than two doses. It's not good for you."

"I'll do my best. Does this mean I don't need bandages? Or do you plan on blindfolding me again and then spoon-feeding me dinner?"

"I'd prefer it if you rested your eyes, but I suspect the rest of us would have a headache from all the griping if I tried to bandage you again. So, dim light only, and don't rub your eyes."

"Thank you." She scooted to the edge of the med bed and kissed G'arn's cheek, earning herself a low *kyrnn* of pleasure.

"It is my pleasure to take care of you," G'arn murmured and nuzzled her neck. "Now and always."

"That almost sounded like a long-term plan, lover." Her pulse raced as G'arn raised his head and she found herself staring into his quicksilver eyes.

"It was." His eyes glowed softly and he cupped her chin in his hand. "*Vardi* does not just mean beloved. It can also mean mate. That is what I want you to be, Layla. That is what I have always wanted."

"But your species bond for life. How can we, if I am with the others, too?

"We'll find a way. But I do not need your answer now. This is new to us all. But now you know what I want from you. Even if this day had not come, I would have pursued you when next we returned home."

"You've turned all of us inside out and upside-down," Mace noted with amusement, his big frame leaning up against the med bay door. "My nice, orderly ship is in chaos, brat."

Layla ignored Mace's teasing as she leaned in and kissed G'arn, her arms twining around his neck as she drew him closer and tangled her tongue with his. He *kyrnned* again, and the soft vibration resonated right through to her soul. When their lips parted she nuzzled into his embrace and breathed deeply so his warm, spicy scent filled her lungs.

"I won't give you an answer yet, G'arn, it's too soon. But I think you should keep calling me *vardi*. I like the way it sounds."

"As do I." He pressed one last kiss to her mouth before stepping away.

Layla released G'arn and looked over at Mace. "And as for you, chief." She winked at him. "If you think you have chaos now, wait until we try to figure out sleeping arrangements. Or do you think we're all going to fit in my quarters?"

Mace groaned. "That conversation is going to have to wait until after I've eaten. I don't know about you, but I am starv—" Alarms clanged and chattered and the med bay was suddenly full of strobing red and amber lights that hurt her eyes. What the hell was wrong?

Mace raced for the nearest computer station, slapped his hand down on a scanner, and barked out an override code she couldn't make out over the wailing of the alarms. A few seconds later, blessed silence returned, but the lights continued to flash in warning.

"What now?" She hopped off the bed and headed for the door.

"We've lost the shield amplifiers in half the sectors and more are going down by the minute," he told her, his expression grim.

"*Re'veth*, a cascade failure? That's bad."

The ship was shielded at all times, a necessity in deep space where even the smallest micro-meteor or radiation source could fry circuits or the crew. The onboard shield generators were old and produced a relatively weak field, in fact they should have been replaced, but instead Torex, the corporation they worked for, had opted for a short-term fix, small amplifiers that boosted the generators' output. The amplifiers were notoriously temperamental, but they could usually be repaired quickly enough, so long as there wasn't any immediate threat. Like, say, a massive cosmic storm.

They were due to be crossing into the worst part of the storm soon. If they didn't fix the shields by the time they lost the protection of the asteroid, they'd all die.

Knowing time was of the essence, Layla headed for the door, but Mace waved her back.

"Hold on a second. We're already pretty deep into the storm. I need to make sure the route to the command deck is still shielded or we'll all be cooked long before we get to where we can do any good."

"I can help with that." G'arn held up an injector. "I need to calculate the dosage, but I should be able to inoculate us against at least some exposure."

"Good. Be sure to bring more of that with you, Tero and Jax are going to need it," Mace said and then swore as he fished out his comms. "Jax, Tero, tell me you're somewhere with shielding right now."

"We're safe, chief," Jax's voice came over the

speaker and Layla let out a breath she hadn't realized she'd been holding. "At least, we're safe for the moment. Crew quarters are deep in the ship, so we've got plenty of hull between us and the interstellar murder storm out there. But we can't get to the bridge from here. Too many unshielded sectors, and that part of the ship is next to the outer hull."

"You two stay put. I'm sending G'arn with something to help counteract the radiation."

"What are you going to do, chief? Can you get to the bridge from the medical bay? Will your medi-bots protect you?" Tero's deep voice was thick with concern.

Mace called up the ship's schematics and cursed. One look at his stormy expression and she knew his answer. There wasn't enough shielding to protect him. Mace was one of the earlier cyborg designs—his medi-bots weren't as advanced as the later models.

"*I* can't. We can use the maintenance shafts, but it's going to be a tight fit," Mace said, his eyes never leaving her.

He was asking her to use the narrow tunnels that ran the length and breadth of the ship to get to the bridge, and she'd have to go alone. They were cramped, grimy, narrow spaces that would barely accommodate her. There was no way the others could fit. G'arn was a good medic, but he could no more repair the shield amplifiers than Layla could diagnose *Traffallian* pox. She was the only one who could do it.

Layla nodded. "I'll go."

Both Tero and Jax bellowed into their comm units at the same time. Apparently, they were opposed to the idea.

"No way are you sending her up there alone!" Jax raged.

"It's not safe!" Tero roared. "You can't ask her!"

"He didn't ask me, I'm volunteering." Layla stretched the truth slightly. Mace hadn't actually said the words, but she'd known what he'd intended anyway. "I'm the only one who can fit. You both know that, so stop arguing. G'arn doesn't know a circuit board from a bowl of oatmeal, so there's no point in him going. Besides, he needs to get to the two of you and make sure you're inoculated. It has to be me."

"*Veth*, I hate this!" Jax snarled, and Layla knew she'd won. Not that they could have stopped her, but this way they wouldn't keep arguing with her while she slowly crawled her way up the ship. An idea started to take root in her mind and she ran with it, ignoring whatever Tero was saying on the comms.

"Chief, can you reprogram the grav plates from here?" she asked as she headed to an inner wall, one with an access hatch to the maintenance shafts.

"I should be able to, why?" Mace asked, still

manning the computer station. "Haven't you had enough fun with gravity the last few days?"

"Just don't put any hot soup in the shaft with me and I should be fine." She found the hatches access panel and it opened with a tap of her fingers. "It just occurred to me that I need to crawl up a *fraxxing* lot of levels, and it would go faster if I didn't have to fight gravity the whole way."

The hatch opened with a hiss and she leaned in to assess things. Dimly lit, lined with wires and pipes, and definitely too narrow for any of her super-sized crewmates. Well, at least the ladder looked sturdy. Layla tried to step inside, but a hand caught her wrist and an arm wrapped around her waist, pulling her up against a hard body. No, two hard bodies.

"I haven't even inoculated you yet. Are you in that much of a hurry to head into danger?" G'arn moved to her side and brushed a kiss to her temple, then nuzzled her hair. "You will be careful, yes?"

"I will be careful. I've spent more than enough time in your medical bay already." Layla held out her arm, and G'arn pressed the compression-powered injector against her skin and pulled the trigger. The sting hadn't even faded before she was spun around, and Mace's mouth crashed down on hers. Powerful arms wrapped around her and hauled her against his chest as his lips slanted across hers.

When he finally released her, he lowered her to the ground slowly, sky-blue eyes boring into hers. "Come back in one piece, you hear me?"

"Yes, sir." Layla tossed off a salute and stepped back from Mace. "I plan on it. It's nice to know you care though, chief."

He growled something under his breath and shook his head. "This isn't caring. This is me not wanting to do any more paperwork." He tugged her back into his arms for one last kiss and tapped her on the ass. "Get going, before I remember how dangerous this is going to be."

Layla took out her communicator, set it to automatically transmit anything she said, and clipped it to her collar. "I love you all, and I'll be back down here to prove it to you soon," she said, knowing her words would be broadcast to Tero and Jax.

She climbed through the hatch and winced slightly as her thighs twinged in protest. *Serves me right for engaging in an all-day sexual marathon right before a life-or-death crisis. Next time I'll have to check the calendar first.*

She grabbed the closest rung of the ladder and then called out, "Ready when you are."

Her stomach did the familiar flutter and surge as gravity ceased to exist, and then she was half climbing, half soaring through the shaft, headed for the first of many connective tunnels. Even without gravity slowing her down, it was going to take a while to wriggle past some of the larger outcroppings of wires and pipes that filled the space. She just hoped there was enough time left to get the shields repaired before the heart of the storm passed over them and tried to kill them all.

CHAPTER NINE

Tero and Jax were in the galley, drinking coffee and listening to every word from both G'arn and Layla as they made their way to their assigned destinations. G'arn was only a few minutes out, but the Pheran wasn't the one they were worried about.

Tero cracked his knuckles and wished for the thousandth time it was anyone but their lover headed for the command deck right now. Jax had tried to fit in the shaft and nearly gotten stuck in the process, and Tero knew better than to even try. They had to sit this one out.

"I'm here." Layla's voice came over the comm and both men sighed in relief. "And for the record, this is the least amount of fun I've had since coming on board."

"Duly noted. We'll discuss compensation and

bonuses later, if we live that long. How's it looking?" Mace asked and they all waited in silence for her answer.

"I see the problem," she said, finally breaking the wordless wait. "Jax, I'm going to need your help talking me through this."

"You got it, sweetheart. Tell me what you're looking at."

The two of them spoke in technical shorthand, and Tero quickly lost track of the conversation. All that mattered was that they were making progress. His thoughts were interrupted by a thump in the wall, and then an electronic hiss as the access hatch opened, revealing a dusty and unhappy-looking medic.

"That was unpleasant," he stated as he climbed out into the galley. "I don't think those shafts have been cleaned since this ship was built." G'arn waved an injector in the air and Tero presented his arm. "I made a double dose for you, Tero."

Jax just held out his arm absently, still talking with Layla. "...third board over, check the second set of relays."

The conversation went on for what seemed like an age, leaving Tero to think about the woman currently trying to save all their lives while risking her own. She wasn't simply crew anymore, and she was far more than a lover. She was what had been missing from the ship, and their lives.

He was small, by the standards of his father's race, and too big for most human women to consider as a lover. Caught between two standards, he'd never really believed he would find a woman who would accept him, not until Layla had looked up at him today and told him she loved him. The fates couldn't bring her into his life and take it all away the same day, could they? *Veth*, he hoped not. If he lost her...if they lost her, none of them would ever be the same.

A whoop of triumph called him back to the present. "Got it! All right, guys, we're safe. Just give it a few minutes for the system to power up, and we should be good to go." There was a note of strain in her voice and Tero used his own comm for the first time.

"Little one, are you all right?"

Her response took too long, the silent seconds speaking volumes before she finally answered. "Just a little dizzy."

G'arn's skin turned two shades darker with worry as he asked, "How long have you been feeling like that?"

"Ten minutes or so? It seems to be getting worse now though."

Dread bloomed deep and cold in the pit of Tero's stomach and he launched himself off his chair, headed for the doors. They didn't open. He tried again, and that's when he saw the red lights of an override command strobe across the top. "Chief! Open the *fraxxing* door!"

"Shields aren't up yet," Layla said, her voice fainter now. "You can charge to my rescue in about two minutes. I'll be fine, big guy. Mace, don't let them out until I give the all clear."

Mace grunted a response, and all three men snarled with frustration. He may have locked them in, but they all knew that grunt.

No doubt he was already on his way to the bridge.

"Jax!" Tero bellowed. "Get your ass over here and help me get this damned door open, now."

"Corbin, I want a status update!" Mace was barking at her, but it was getting hard to focus.

It was like she'd spent all her energy getting the repair done, and now it was easier to drift. Still, he *was* her boss. She mustered the last of her reserves and spoke. "Shield amplifiers are recharging and will be back online shortly, sir."

"That's not the status I want an update on."

What else was there?

Layla closed her eyes and concentrated on getting

the words out. "I'm not doing as well as the shields, but we're both hanging in there."

"I meant what I said earlier. I'm not doing any more paperwork, so you just hold on until we can get to you."

It was nice to know they all cared so much. Who knew a bunch of hard-ass miners could be so sweet? Not that she was going to say so to their handsome faces. They'd just deny it anyway. The thoughts she was having made her laugh, and she curled up on the floor by the console she'd been working on and relaxed.

Her arms ached from hauling herself through the shaft, and she was cold despite the fact that she was sweating.

I've got radiation sickness. The thought drifted through her mind and she sighed inwardly. It looked like Mace was going to have to do some paperwork after all. "Sorry boss," she mumbled and curled her legs up tighter against her chest.

"Damn it, Corbin! I'm sure I gave you an order about staying in one piece!" She fumbled for the comm wondering why it was suddenly so loud. "Layla, open your eyes for me." She groggily realized Mace was here, and she fought to get her eyes open, but her eyelids were so heavy it was all she could do to crack them a little, just enough to make out Mace's frowning face.

"Are ta shieldss up?"

"They're up. You did it. Now, let's get you to medical. G'arn is going to want to have a look at you."

"Only if you let 'im out outta ta galley," she slurred again and frowned as she realized how thick her speech had gotten. "I'm not doin' so good."

"No, you're not." Mace brushed a hand over her forehead. "You've gone and disobeyed another order, Corbin. This is getting to be a habit!"

"I'm shtill in one piece!"

"Put your arms around my neck and I'll get you to G'arn."

She reached for him, and the moment he had her in his arms, she closed her eyes again. It was too much work to keep them open any longer. Her ears still worked fine though, and it wasn't long before she heard the pounding of boots coming up the corridor at a run and Mace sighing.

"Bet ta galley door's toast."

"No bet. But they're going to pay for it out of their bonus."

Voices jabbered, questions were asked and somewhere in the middle of it all she lost her grip on the world and it slid away from her, leaving her drifting in the dark.

WHEN SHE WOKE AGAIN, the voices were still there, buzzing and muttering.

"...we're all in agreement then?" Mace asked.

The others all made noises of approval, and she wondered what they were discussing. "Guys?" Her voice was raspy, and her mouth was parched, but she managed to keep talking. "Whatever you're voting on can wait. Your conquering heroine wants her accolades now." She opened her eyes slowly and the faces of her males came into focus, all of them wearing expressions of concern.

"Welcome back, little one." Tero tucked her hand into his much larger one and squeezed her fingers.

"I'm getting tired of having to visit you in the medical bay. Will you do us all a favor and quit getting hurt?" Jax took her other hand and laced his fingers through hers.

"You're generating way too much paperwork for a lowly technician," Mace chimed in.

"And running through my medical supply inventory at an alarming rate," G'arn added, a faint smile playing at his lips.

"So much for accolades. I guess this means no raise either?"

"Raise? You've been asleep for two days, Corbin.

I'm seriously considering putting you on report for failing to report to work!" Mace leaned over her and brushed a kiss to her cheek. "But since you saved all our asses, I'm giving you a pass, just this once."

"Two days?" Layla croaked and sat up. "I've been out two *days*? I thought it was a few minutes!"

"Your body needed time to heal, and I knew if I tried to order you to stay in bed and rest, you'd be on your feet and causing havoc." G'arn dropped his shoulder in his version of a shrug. "So I kept you sedated."

"You *drugged* me?" Layla asked in disbelief and then turned on the others. "And you lot let him?"

"The only reason you survived was because of that injection I gave you, combined with the healing accelerator already in your body. The entire bridge was being bombarded by cosmic radiation, and you along with it. It was a near thing, *vardi*. We almost lost you."

"But I'm going to be fine now, right? No lasting damage? No risk of growing a second head?"

"I'll need to keep an eye on you for a while, and when we get back to civilized space I'm going to recommend you have a cellular level scan to ensure there's nothing I missed, but yes, I believe you will be fine." G'arn smiled in reassurance. "And your eyes have now had proper time to heal as well, which I am pleased about."

"You are a very sneaky male." She stuck out her tongue at G'arn, who responded with a low, sexy growl that made her quiver. "So, I'm cleared to go back to work?"

"No." Mace shook his head. "Not until tomorrow."

"Good. Then I vote we go to the galley and you can feed me the two days' worth of meals I missed."

"The guys have been cooking all day, so we'll go eat soon. We've got something we want to talk to you about first." Mace looked as serious as she'd ever seen him, and Layla stayed silent, waiting to hear what he had to say.

"The thing is, we've been pooling our money for years so we could buy this ship and become independent operators. Jax and I were partners from the beginning and the others have joined us along the way. This has been a long-term goal of ours, and when we're done this trip, we'll have enough to make the deal." He stopped and scrubbed a hand across his jaw. "We want to make this a five-way partnership. You in?"

Layla opened her mouth to answer, but Jax spoke first, his tone full of laughter. "And so speaks our fearless leader. Way to put your heart into it, chief." He raised Layla's hand to his lips and kissed her fingers before continuing. "What he meant to say was that we love you, and we've had plenty of time to think about what you meant to us while you were healing. We want you to stay with us, Layla. Not just for this trip, or for a contract. We want you to stay forever."

"But I don't have the money to buy in."

"You risked your life to save all of ours. I think that's worth more than scrip. We all do." Tero stepped closer to her bedside. "We'll have the money soon, that's taken care of. We just want you to say yes to being a partner once we own this ship. That way, the five of us will officially be together. "

"You're my *vardi*, Layla. I know you are. I believe you are all of our *vardi*. Our life mate." G'arn placed his hand on her thigh, his thumb moving in slow circles and distracting her from thinking about anything other than how good it felt when he touched her. When they were all touching her.

"If I stayed—if I became a partner—this wouldn't be just business. This would be us taking what we started the other day and making it permanent."

"I thought I said that already," Mace grumbled. "Was I not clear?"

"You really aren't any good at the mushy stuff, are you, chief?" Layla laughed and reclaimed her hands so she could hold them out to Mace. "Tell me why you want me to stay, and I'll say yes."

"Brat." He took her hands and drew her into his arms. "I want you to stay because this place has been more of a home since you came to us than it ever was before. You're meant to be here, with us. We're better with you here. *I'm* better for having you here. And there's the whole matter of the fact I'm in love with you, but you knew that already."

"I will never get tired of hearing it, though. "Her heart swelled with joy and love as she looked at them. "So, I'll want to hear it often, from all of you."

"I think we can manage that," Jax said, beaming. "Does that mean you're staying?"

"Yes, I'm staying. Where else in the galaxy am I going to find anyone who could compare to the four of you?" She found herself caught up in a smothering hug as all her lovers converged around her bed kissing her and whispering their love before leaving her with G'arn.

"Before you dismiss me from your care, I have a favor to ask." She tipped her head back to stare into his silver eyes. "Actually, I have two. First, I'd like to use your shower again."

"Yes, of course." G'arn nodded, a smile on his lips. "And what else can I do for my *vardi*?"

Layla brushed her fingertips over his lips, loving the silken heat of his skin. "You can join me."

CHAPTER TEN

G'ARN DIDN'T WASTE a moment of their time alone. His cock swelled to life so quickly it bordered on painful as he gathered Layla into his arms and carried her to the small cleansing unit. He hadn't been able to forget how she had looked the last time she'd used his shower. The image of her silhouetted against the glass had haunted his fantasies for the past two days.

He stripped away her clothes, exposing her pale gold skin and the pert globes of her breasts. Unable to resist, he bowed his head and suckled one nipple into his mouth, craving the taste and the feel of her. This time it was just the two of them, and his need to claim her quickly warred with the desire to indulge in this moment when it was just the two of them.

She buried her hands in his hair, pulling him closer as she rubbed herself across the front of his body. Need spiked through him, raw and sharp, and he knew they would have to take it slowly another time, but not today.

He nipped her breast lightly and then stood, taking a half step back so he had room to strip away his own clothes. She helped, undoing his pants and drawing them down his legs with an urgency that mirrored his own. His arms were still tangled in his shirt when her mouth closed around his cock, sending a bolt of lust sizzling through his veins. *Re'veth*, she had a talented tongue.

He managed to get the shirt off and tossed it away, one hand gripping the door to the shower to keep his balance as she took as much of his dick as she could into the soft warmth of her mouth. "I want to be inside you when I come," he protested. "I need to be inside you."

Her only answer was a low hum that vibrated down his shaft to his balls and made him *kyrnn* in response. Primal need pushed aside logic and ran roughshod over every thought but the drive to have her and claim her for his own. He pulled her to her feet and stepped out of his pants as he backed her into the shower stall, pressed up against her so she was pinned to the wall. Skin to skin at last, he hit the shower's on switch blindly and took her mouth in a punishing kiss she answered in kind.

He slid a hand between them, tracing down her body to the apex of her thighs and then pressed between them to cup her pussy against his palm. She ground herself against his fingers, letting him between her already slick lips as hot water streamed down over them both, fanning the flames of their need ever higher.

Her clit was a hot, swollen knot buried in her folds and he worked it with his fingers, stroking and pinching by turns as she moaned and shuddered at every touch. This was his mate, hot, eager and wanting, and his every instinct was screaming at him to claim her for now and always.

"Give yourself to me, Layla," he worked the words past the tightness of his throat.

"Yes." She moaned and looked up at him, brown eyes soft and glowing with emotions he had never seen in her before. Love, tenderness and adoration. "You are my *vardo*, as I am your *vardi*."

She knew the ritual words. He was stunned and honored she had learned so much about his culture, but those thoughts were fleeting as his instincts screamed to the fore and it was time to claim her.

"This is forever," he whispered and removed his hand from her pussy to cup her ass, hauling her up against him.

"I know. Mark me already." She smirked up at him

and he lost the battle for control. He lifted her into his arms, barely waiting for her to wrap her legs around his waist before he slammed his cock deep into the slick heat of her pussy and held her so they were skin to skin, inside and out. His tongue thrust and tangled with hers and her low moans were almost a match for the steady rumble of his *kyrnning* as their two bodies became one.

Her thighs clamped around his hips and she lifted herself up enough he had room to move and he took it. Hard and fast, his hips rocked and bucked into her, driving both of them into a frenzy of need.

When she came, her walls clenched around him so tightly starbursts exploded across his vision, and his balls all but turned inside out as jet after jet of his seed filled her body, marking her forever as his. Pheremones filled the air, dousing them both and completing his claiming. She was his. That knowledge made every tremor and touch even better, and he held her to him long after he was spent, enjoying the moment of completeness.

"We're going to get waterlogged if we stay here much longer." It was Layla who finally broke the silence, lifting her head from his shoulder with a contented sigh. "And I still need to wash my hair and clean up."

"I will wash you, my love. It will always be my

pleasure to take care of you." He helped her untangle her limbs from his, parting their bodies with reluctance. "My *vardi*." He kissed her again, and in his mind she already tasted subtly different, she tasted of him.

Every Pheran male would know immediately she was his. As he gently massaged the soap into her hair, he couldn't stop grinning. He had his life mate, and she would be staying on board with the rest of his family, forever.

G'ARN HAD WASHED every inch of her, leaving her tingling and feeling well loved by the time they joined the others in the galley. Once there, Layla had been surprised to discover they had made every single one of her favorite foods and had even managed to coax a passable chocolate mousse out of the normally temperamental food dispenser. They hadn't let her raise a finger to help, and she'd enjoyed playing queen to her host of eager knights. She could definitely get used to this.

After eating, they all adjourned to the rec area, and Layla burst into a fit of giggles as something struck her. "So, if this is all here," she waved toward the makeshift bed they'd created. "Does this mean you've all been sleeping together?"

"Let's not put it that way, shall we?" Jax grumbled and swatted her ass cheek. "And for the record, nothing in the known galaxy snores as loudly as a Torski sleeping on his back."

"I don't snore!" Tero muttered.

"Yes, you do!" the other three men barked in unison and Layla laughed, overcome with joy and a sense of rightness. This was what it was going to be like from now on, the five of them fighting, loving, and sharing everything.

"So where do I sleep?" She walked around the outside of the massive bed.

"The middle, of course." Jax winked at her. "Easy access." And just like that, he had her in his arms, crushing her lips with his as he lifted her off her feet and kissed her deeply.

"Engineers, always have to have their hands on everything!" Mace complained and when Layla glanced around and saw the guys busy stripping out of their clothes, eager to join in. That was all she got to see before Jax kissed her again and stole her breath away with a kiss that sent sparks shimmering over her skin. Hands tugged at her pants, sliding them down over her legs and she heard a hiss of appreciation as they fell away and her lovers all realized she'd forgone underwear again.

"New orders, Corbin. I want you to start wearing underwear, at least when we're working. If we think you're going around bare-assed, none of us are going to have our minds on the job. I sure as *fraxx* won't."

"That's going to be a problem, chief." She kicked herself free of her pants before glancing back over her shoulder at Mace. "I didn't actually pack any."

She yelped as Mace moved in behind her and swatted her bare ass with his hand. "Our work efficiency just went out the airlock."

"We're screwed," Tero muttered in agreement. "To think she's been working with us half-naked all this time…"

"And fantasizing about us naked the other half." Jax loosened his hold on her and started drawing her shirt up over her head.

"Six months, wasted," G'arn sighed.

"It wasn't wasted. It gave us time to get to know each other. Now we just need to spend the next six months making up for lost time." Layla felt another pair of arms encircle her and a set of large hands covered her breasts, drawing her up against a hot-skinned male. Tero held her, his thick cock pressed along her spine as the others settled themselves onto the mattress with G'arn stretched up in the middle.

"Come here, *vardi*." G'arn patted high on his chest and Tero simply lifted her off her feet and lowered her so she straddled G'arn's face, his breath fanning over her pussy.

"Yes," he hissed with pleasure and curled his hands around her hips, drawing her down against his mouth as he burrowed into her pussy eagerly. His mouth latched onto her clit and Layla nearly screamed with pleasure as the low rumble of his arousal transformed his entire mouth into a vibrator. Her clit throbbed and swelled as he suckled and lashed it with his tongue, and it was all she could do to remember to breathe.

"Does that feel good?" Mace asked from his vantage point to one side. She nodded, watching as he stroked his dick with one hand. "Is he making your pussy wet, Layla? I hope so, because once he makes you come, I'm going to fuck that hot little pussy and Jax is going to fuck your ass, and we're going to make you come again.

"Tero." She groaned his name and he appeared in front of her, dropping one hand to cradle her head.

"Yeah, he needs you, too. Do you think you could suck him while G'arn eats you out?" Mace's voice was huskier now, and both he and Jax had their cocks in a firm grip, pumping their shafts as they watched her and G'arn.

Layla reached for Tero, wrapping her fingers

around his thick length as she leaned forward to swipe her tongue over the tip. He groaned and moved in closer, and a few drops of moisture appeared, tempting her to taste him again. This time she swirled her tongue over the head and her mouth filled with the taste of cloves, hot and vaguely sweet.

He was too big to fit in her mouth, and the way G'arn was working over her clitoris had her panting for breath so quickly she wouldn't have been able to anyway, so instead she wrapped both hands around Tero's cock and focused her attention on the head, lapping and sucking as she worked his impressive length with her hands.

"*Veth*, yes!" He growled and slowly rocked his hips. "Just like that, little one."

The three of them found a rhythm, letting their pleasure flow between them like an endless river. Too soon, G'arn had her on the jagged edge of her control, and she had to fight to stop herself from coming before Tero did.

G'arn sensed she was resisting him and growled, nipping at her tender clit. That sharp pleasure-pain pushed her past her limits and sent her into climax. Tero's cock muffled the sounds of her cries as she bucked and writhed against G'arn's mouth, and then Tero groaned and arched his back as he came, pumping his essence down Layla's throat.

Jax hadn't realized voyeurism was one of his kinks, but watching Layla finding her pleasure with the others made him so hard and horny it was obvious, now. "*Fraxx*, that's better than any sim, ever. Was that good for you, sweetheart?"

Layla released Tero's cock and nodded. "So good."

"Good, because we're about to make you do that again. You ready?" Jax asked, already imagining how good it would feel to be inside her again.

She looked up at him with an eager smile that had his cock throbbing. "Oh, yeah." She looked down at G'arn. "I'm good to go, right?"

G'arn nodded. "I cleared you for full activity. Work *and* play. So, unless you're not feeling like coming again..."

"I'm not sure my heart can take it, but I'm willing to take the risk."

Jax knew she was joking, but he needed to make something clear. "You know we'd never risk losing you, sweetheart. Not again. I think we'd all rather die than go through that again."

"I'd do it again in a heartbeat. If I hadn't, we wouldn't be here right now. I just got my wish granted, no way I'm giving that up any time soon."

Her legs were still trembling as she got to her feet.

Tero and G'arn moved in quickly, helping her into position so she straddled his body with her back to him, his cock rising up just behind her. He took a moment to apply a generous amount of barrier gel to his cock then coaxed her up and forward so he could do the same to her pretty little ass.

Mace knelt between Jax's thighs, then pulled Layla even farther forward so he could kiss her while Jax took advantage of her new position to start teasing her with his fingers. He parted her ass cheeks and stroked one lubed finger over her anus while Mace reached between her legs to toy with her slick pussy.

She moaned and rocked her hips, asking for more, but neither of them sped up. He didn't need to speak to Mace to know they were on the same page. They wanted her wild with need when they took her. He planned on continuing his slow, gentle touches until her legs were shaking and begging them for release.

It didn't take them long to get her there. Soon she was rocking between them, panting and trembling as they worked in concert to bring her as much pleasure as they could. She was so damned beautiful this way, flushed and wild, a creature of pure passion. He didn't know what they could have done to deserve a woman like Layla, but he was grateful the universe had brought her into their orbit.

"You are so damned sexy, sweetheart. I am never going to get tired of watching you like this."

G'arn and Tero murmured in agreement, and even Mace managed to hum an approving note without breaking his lip lock with their lover.

They worked together, until she finally tore her mouth from Mace's to growl in frustration, and shoved her hips backward, impaling herself on Jax's fingers.

"I think she's trying to tell us something." He worked his fingers in deeper, stretching her so she could accommodate more of him.

"I suspect if you don't move things along, she may just start inflicting random damage on you both," G'arn observed from his side of the bed.

She glanced back over her shoulder to meet Jax's eyes. "G'arn's right. If you two don't stop teasing and fuck me, I'm going to get violent."

"My momma always wanted me to settle down with a sweet, lovable girl." Jax withdrew his fingers and pressed the head of his cock against her tight hole. "And I went and fell for a *peskin* instead."

Before she could react to his taunt, he pressed himself past the tight ring of muscles and into her body. Whatever she was going to say vanished in a wordless moan as she wriggled her hips, taking him deeper.

"So tight. Damn you feel good, sweetheart. Now, if

you ease yourself back. Yes, just like that." He groaned loudly. All the air left his lungs as her body squeezed his cock like a vice and she stretched out across his chest. He reached around to cup her breasts as she parted her thighs and opened herself to Mace.

Being inside her, holding her tight while Mace moved to claim her was the most intimate, incredible moment of his life, and Jax would do whatever it took to make this magic between them last forever.

THE REALITY of being with all of them was so much more than anything Laya had dared to dream of, and she loved every second of it.

"You look incredible laid out like this." Mace stroked a finger over her clit and then flicked it lightly. "You ready for me?"

"Yes!" She tried to wriggle closer to Mace's cock but all she accomplished was to drive Jax deeper, making them both groan. That was the moment Mace finally took her, arching over her as he eased his cock deep into her channel, filling her completely and pinning her against Jax with the weight of his body. Mace's mouth brushed over hers, their breath mingling as he gave her a moment to adjust.

"Tell me this feels as good for you as it does for me," he panted.

In answer, she flexed her inner walls, clamping her body around them both.

"*Veth*, that's good. Do it again, sweetheart." Jax bucked his hips and she did it again, earning a groan from them both. Jax's hands slipped under Mace to cup Layla's breasts, his calloused fingers tweaking her nipples as they worked out a rhythm between them. There was nothing Layla could do but accept their claiming, caught between two of her lovers and carried ever upward, closer and closer to bliss.

She knew G'arn and Tero were watching because she could feel their eyes on her with every breath and cry, and the rightness of having them all around her, all with her, made her heart swell with love. That thought was what sent her over the edge and into a whirlwind of need and pleasure, too far gone in her own orgasm to even know which of her guys came next.

She only knew they were not far behind her, all of them crying out in release and then slumping over each other in blissful exhaustion as the last tremors and aftershocks finally passed.

Mace moved first, and gentle hands coaxed her off of Jax and settled her onto the bed they now all shared. Layla didn't even open her eyes, she just snuggled into the warmth and comfort of whoever was behind her. Soon she was surrounded by her lovers, and the sound of their breathing was the most comforting thing she'd ever known.

This was the family she had always wanted and never imagined she would find. She loved them all for different reasons, and they returned her love fourfold. Six months ago, when she'd signed onto the crew of the *Kessel Queen*, she would have bet against her finding love out here in the darkness between the stars. That was a bet she was happy to have lost.

EPILOGUE - SIX MONTHS LATER

MACE LOOKED around the table at his family and felt a surge of smug satisfaction. It had taken another half-year of hard work and dedication to both the job and each other, but they had done it. To celebrate, they were taking a night off to drink and dine at one of the nicer clubs on this part of the Drift, the Nova Club. He raised his mug and toasted the others. "Here's to hard work, trust, and our official partnership. The *Queen* is ours. From now on, we chart our own course!"

Everyone cheered and raised their glass in return. Once it was quiet, Layla rose from her seat beside him and raised her glass again. "And here's to the success of our new *family* business."

That brought another round of cheers, this one even louder than the first. They'd finalized the paperwork on the Kessel Queen this afternoon, but yesterday they'd closed an even more important deal, locking Layla into a lifelong contract as their wife. They were a family, now. One bound together by love, chaos, and dysfunction, but a family, nevertheless.

They'd gotten married in a quick, quiet civil ceremony here on Astek Station. He'd expected some reaction to the news the five of them wanted to get married, but the clerk had only smiled, handed them each a data pad with the legal documentation, and wished them a joyful union. It was one of the reasons he liked working this far from the more 'civilized' parts of the galaxy. The beings here were all just trying to get by, which didn't leave as much time for judgement or discrimination.

Layla rose from the table and walked around, kissing each of them all along the way. When she reached Mace, he didn't settle for a kiss, though. He hauled her into his arms and onto his lap, his mouth mated to hers.

"Hey!" She protested when she finally pulled away and leaned toward her empty seat with outstretched arms. "I can't reach my drink from here."

"Someone get our wife her drink."

"G'arn leaned over to hand it to her. "There you are."

"Thank you, husband." She beamed at G'arn.

G'arn actually blushed, his cheeks darkening to almost midnight blue. "My pleasure, *vardi*."

"Husbands and wife. I'm still not used to hearing those words, but damn, I like them," Jax said.

A large male clad in Nova Club uniform walked by during their conversation. He stopped and turned toward their table. "Excuse me, did I hear that right? You're newly married? All of you?"

Mace held Layla a little tighter as the others all turned to the new arrival.

"We made it official yesterday," Layla said, flashing the ring they'd bought for her.

The big man smiled. "Congratulations! Next round is on the house. These days, all good news should be celebrated."

"Thank you." Mace stuck out his left hand since his right was wrapped around Layla. He kept it turned so the barcode wasn't visible. "I'm Mace, and this is my family—Layla, G'arn, Tero, and Jax."

"Nice to meet you." The male took his hand, shook it, and turned wrist to expose Mace's barcode. He grinned. "I thought so. Welcome to the Nova Club, brother. I'm Kit Armas, and this is my club." He let go of Mace's hand and flashed his own barcode.

"Yours?" Mace took a look around the bustling

space and whistled. "Nice to see a some of us are doing well. The last time I was on this station, this club and everything else was just starting up. That was a couple of years ago, though."

"Yeah, because we've been saving our scrip, which meant staying away from the temptations of places like this." Tero gestured to encompass the sleek bar stocked with liquor from all over the galaxy, the gaming tables, and the throng of customers enjoying every entertainment money could buy.

"My batch siblings and I own the place, and yeah, business has really taken off. Our wife helps, too, but she's expecting twins any day now, so she's not supposed to be working."

Layla laughed. "And how's that going?"

Kit grinned and shrugged. "About as well as you'd think." He tipped his head to a table in the VIP section, where a female with blue hair and skin was seated, talking to several human women. "That's our girl, Zura, over there."

"Congratulations on the pending arrival of twins. You seem pretty calm for a soon-to-be father," Mace said.

Another male joined Kit, and for a second Mace thought he was seeing double. The men were identical. "This is my brother, Luke. Luke, can you find these folk's tab and add a round on the house? They just got married yesterday." He nodded to Mace. "And Mace here is one of us."

"Yeah?" Luke grinned. "Congrats, and welcome to the Nova." He lowered his voice. "You here because of the rumors?"

Mace frowned and shook his head, not sure what Luke was referring to. "We're here while our ship is being refitted and repaired. We've been asteroid mining on a year-long contract and just got back. Which rumors are you referring to?"

Luke's grin widened and his voice dropped to a conspirator's whisper. "You don't know?"

"Don't tease them, Luke. It's obvious they haven't heard."

Both men went quiet for a moment, but they maintained eye contact. Mace knew they were talking to each other via the internal comms channels all cyborgs shared with their batch siblings. It had been years since he'd had anyone else on his channel. So long, he'd almost forgotten about it.

Layla stirred in his lap, about to say something, when both men nodded.

"Right. I'll tell them," Luke said.

"And I'll let the others know," Kit replied. "It was nice meeting all of you. I'm sure we'll talk again, soon."

Luke looked around at them all. "Come with me.

You've just got an upgrade to the VIP Section. Grab your drinks and I'll fill you in."

Mace grudgingly set Layla back on her feet, gathered up their drinks, and followed the others through the crowd. Luke led them to a seat near the back, spoke a few words to a server, and joined them.

"You missed a lot. I'll hit the highlights for you."

"We were only gone a year," Mace said.

"Is this related to why there are so many IAF soldiers on what's supposed to be a recreation station?" Layla added.

Luke started talking, and within a few minutes they were all listening with rapt interest as he detailed what had happened while they were out of contact. They'd heard a few rumors, but most of what they'd heard seemed too insane to be believed."

When Luke was done, they all stared at him in amazement. "We were only gone a *vething* year," Jax muttered.

Mace was still trying to wrap his head around it all when Layla spoke up. "These medi-bots. The ones that don't need a genetic match. If a normal being got injected with them, would they live longer? Like, say, as long as a cyborg?"

Their host nodded. "We think so. No one knows how long a cyborg's lifespan is, though, so it's not a sure thing."

"But it's going to be longer than a human's," she said, and it finally sunk in what she was getting at.

Mace had been so busy enjoying his time with Layla, it hadn't dawned on him that he'd outlive her... and everyone else he cared about. He would be alone again someday. Alone, and grieving.

Luke glanced over to where his wife was sitting and nodded. "We're going to live a long time. Centuries, even. I can't imagine how Kit and I would deal with knowing Zura wouldn't be with us for every moment. Fortunately, we don't have to face that problem."

"Wait. Your wife carries those medi-bots?" Mace asked. The female was pregnant, which meant – *Re'veth*. It meant everything was about to change.

"She actually carries our medi-bots. Long story. But yeah, she's going to live a long time, and so will our kids. They'll be born with nanotech, and now the cyborg females can have children again, change is coming."

"Big changes," G'arn said, his silver eyes wide.

"If the five of you think you want to be part of that change, you could sign up to get the medi-bot injections. We're not supposed to talk about it, but..." Luke shrugged. "We're not fond of secrets around here, and the more beings who know about this, the less likely the corporations or the IAF can make it all disappear."

"There's a list? We could get on it?" Layla was almost vibrating with eagerness, and Mace stroked her hair in a vain attempt to calm her.

"There is. See the blonde sitting with Zura? That's Dr. Alyson Jefferies. She's the one who found the cure for the female cyborgs. She's got a list of interested parties. Between the IAF and the corporations, you'll have to fill out enough paperwork to fill a shuttle hangar, but if you're interested—"

Layla didn't let him utter another word. "Hell yeah, I'm interested. My biggest nightmare is knowing we're not all going to age at the same rate. Eventually, Mace would be left alone. If there's a way to stop that from happening, I'm all in, and I bet the rest of my guys are, too."

Every single male at the table nodded.

"We vowed to be together for as long as we all shall live," Tero said. "We can't know how long that will be, but anything that gives us more time together is a good idea."

"What the big guy said," Jax agreed.

"I will treasure every day we have together, *vardi*," G'arn looked at the others. "And I suppose I'd be happier having the rest of you fools around, too."

Mace didn't know what to say, so he didn't try. He just gave the males a shit-eating grin and bowed his head to claim Layla's mouth with his. Today was the best day of his life. After the war, losses, hardships, and years of work, he finally had everything he'd dreamed of, and so much more besides.

None of them knew what the future would bring, but so long as they had Layla in their lives, he knew every day would be a good one, for all of them.

The End

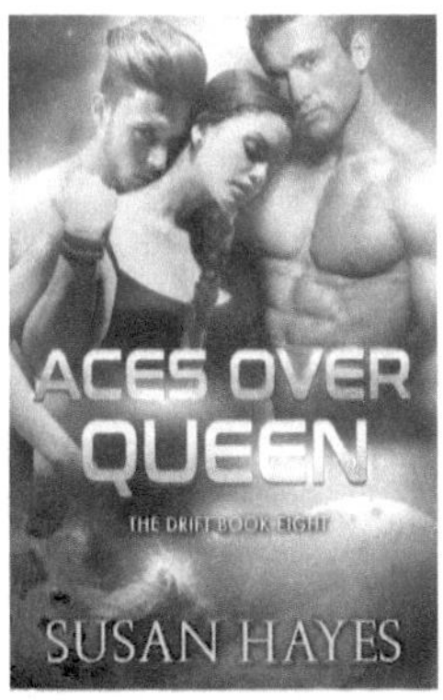

Releasing May 2019

To win their queen's heart, this pair must risk it all.

Royan Watson lived by three simple rules: No regrets, no relationships, and no slowing down. No exceptions. Then steady, reliable, and sexy as hell

Owen Connors crossed his orbit, and Royan's rules went out the airlock.

Astek station is in chaos and it's Tiana Astor's task to set things right. But no briefing could prepare the ice queen of Astek Corp for the Drift's secrets, lies, or the temptations she'll find there.

Coming Soon

Chapter One

Tiana loved the freedom of travelling. It was one of the few times in her life she could relax and be herself. Given the magnitude of her new assignment, this trip to the Drift might be the last time she could relax for quite awhile. Knowing that, she'd requested as small a crew as possible - a flight team and two members of Astek's private security force. Ideally, she would have managed the trip solo, but there wasn't a snowball's chance in a supernova her father would allow that, not right now. Things were too unsettled, too dangerous. The corporations were on uneasy footing. Old alliances were unravelling, the body count was rising, and trust was in short supply.

According to her father, trust was the reason she was headed to the edge of known space to take over control of Astek Station. Callum Astor might doubt her abilities, but her loyalty absolute. He knew she'd do what was needed to protect the family business.

She set aside her mug of tea and stood, indulging in a slow stretch to ease the knots in her neck and shoulders. She'd spent the better part of the day in her quarters, reading about her new home - Astek Station. By the time she arrived, she intended to know everything she could about the station, the people who worked for her, and the ones who might be plotting against her, her father, and the family business.

"Tink. Please remind me to have a new set of blueprints of Astek space station drawn up once we arrive. The ones on file are more than two years out of date."

"Filing reminder, now." The cheerful, airy voice of her virtual assistant replied.

"Thank you, Tink." It drove her father to distraction that she had named her digital assistant after a character in an ancient children's story. It made him even more irritated that she spoke to Tink like it was a sentient being.

"Is there anything else, Tiana? You have worked through your usual mealtime. Shall I order a meal to be delivered to your quarters?"

"That sounds perfect. I'll have my usual and a slice of cherry pie."

"I believe the food dispenser is out of cherry pie. Would you like to substitute apple pie, instead?"

Tiana wrinkled her nose. "We're going to be another week or more in transit. I'm going to be very grumpy if there's no cherry pie until we get to the Drift."

"Noted. Checking inventory now." There was a momentary silence. "I'm sorry, Tiana, because of the change in departure times, some supplies did not make it aboard on time."

She sighed. "Apple pie will be fine, thanks. And you have nothing to apologize for. My father was the one who insisted we left early and post a false destination so no one would know where we were headed, or when." He'd been worried about her safety, which was hard to believe. He rarely worried about anything.

Her father was always calm, controlled, and deliberate. The only time she'd seen him show any signs of emotional distress was the first time she woke up after her accident. He'd be there, sitting by her bed in a rumpled suit, looking haggard and worn in a way she'd never seen before, or since.

There'd been an echo of that distress in his eyes when he'd called her in to give her this assignment.

"This is going to be dangerous, Tiana. If I could keep you here, I would, but there's too much at risk. Be careful who you trust. We have enemies who might be emboldened by everything that's going on.

"Astek station needs a strong hand to bring it back in line, and you'll have to do it without upsetting the Interstellar Armed Forces, Nova Force, our allies, or the factions already present on the station. I know this this might be too much for you, but you're the only one I can trust to protect the family's interests."

His dismissal of her abilities had stung. They always did, but she'd learned to use the pain. It drove her to work harder, to be better. That drive had helped her recover from the crash, too.

Recollections of the battle she'd waged to reclaim her life made her body ache with remembered pain. "Tink, run a shower for me, will you. I should have time before my meal gets here."

"Your shower is now running. Your meal will be ready in fifteen minutes. Would you like me to inform you when it has arrived?"

"I would. Thanks, Tink."

Tianna stripped off her clothes as she walked, dropping them on the floor just for the amusement of watching the housekeeping bots scuttle out of their charging stations to tidy up the trail of abandoned clothing.

The moment she opened the door to the sanitation room she was enveloped in a cloud of fragrant steam. Oranges, she guessed, with a hint of something spicy underneath. Tink selected the scents using its database of aromatherapy information, and somehow it always seemed to find the right fragrance to suit her mood.

She stepped under the stream of hot water, letting the heat penetrate her body. There was always a strange moment when her artificial parts took a few extra moments to warm up, and she could feel the difference, a slight chill in her limbs and at the back of her skull. The sensation passed quickly, but it served as a daily reminder of how close she'd come to death, and what had been done to keep her alive.

She ran a sudsy hand down her body, doing a silent inventory of her injuries. The surgeons had done immaculate work, leaving her skin with barely a scar or blemish. The real changes were invisible from the outside. Her bones had been shattered. Her organs ruptured, her limbs crushed and mangled beyond recognition. The skimmer crash left her with catastrophic injuries.

Unsurvivable. That's what it said in her file. But she had survived. All it took was money, connections, and a corporate tycoon who would rather break galactic law, as well as the laws of nature, than lose his only heir.

What she might have wanted had never even been a factor.

When the first explosion tore through the ship, she thought she was having a flashback to the crash. The impression only lasted a split second. When the second, larger explosion hit, she was tossed around the tiny shower space, slamming into the walls several times before crashing to the floor. It couldn't have been more than a few seconds, but she experienced every moment in slow-motion. She was airborne. The lights flickered. Impact. Airborne again. The lights went out. Warning alarms screamed. A flash of red. Impact again. Pain. Fear. Another moment of flight. She tumbled again, crashing headlong into something. The tumbling stopped. There was silence.

When Tianna came to, she was floating. Disoriented and dazed, she reached out wildly, trying to find something to connect with in the dark. Her hand hit a wall, still warm and slick from her shower. Shower. She'd been showering when...something happened. Something big and explode-y.

"*Fraxx*," she swore, her voice a welcome break in the silence. "Tink, If you're there, I could use a status report."

The braided gold band on her left wrist buzzed slightly, confirming Tink's presence. "I am here, though in a diminished capacity. The ship's AI is offline. I am operating on backup power and have limited abilities. I am unable to give you a full assessment at this time."

"Forget the full assessment. Tell me what you know. How bad is it?" Tianna felt her way out of the shower, no easy task when there was no gravity or light to see by.

"The ship is adrift. I am unable to detect any energy output on any deck."

"Life signs?"

"Scanning." Tink was silent for several long, terrible seconds. "I am unable to locate any other life signs in the immediate vicinity. My sensor range is minimal, however. It is possible..."

"We both no that's not likely." Tianna's heart sank. The crew was gone. Killed by whatever had taken out her ship and left her adrift in a crippled wreck.

"What happened?" Something brushed by her face in the dark, and she flinched, swatting it away out of instinct. When her hand touched soft fabric, she realized it was only a towel and grabbed it. She couldn't do much at the moment, but she could get herself dried off.

"I have limited data, but it is eighty-nine percent likely that the ship experienced multiple explosive decompressions in a very small time period."

"You mean the ship blew up. How did it happen?

No, scratch that. It doesn't matter right now. How long can you function on backup power?"

"Forty-nine hours, twelve minutes with minimal output."

That wasn't so bad. "And how long can I survive given the current situation?"

"I do not have enough data to make an accurate calculation."

Dammit, Tink. Give me your best guess. How long do I have?"

"You have less than twenty hours worth of breathable atmosphere. Life support is offline, but it will take some time for the temperature to drop to dangerous levels."

Fraxx. "Has a distress beacon been activated?"

"Affirmative. The beacon is automated and functioning normally."

"Then I guess we better hope someone answers that beacon before I run out of air or freeze to death." Her father's choices might have saved her life, again. A human being would die when the temperature dropped too far, or the carbon dioxide rose too high. She wasn't human, though. Not anymore. She was a cyborg with a body loaded with military grade nanotech whose only purpose was to keep her alive.

In the years since the crash, she'd always played it

safe. No more risks. No adventures. She hadn't tested her medi-bots against anything more dangerous than the occasional flu virus. Now, she was going to push the tech to its limits. And if it failed, she'd die.

Coming Soon